HEAT

Volume 1

Published by Ink & Quill Press, 2026

For more excellent works of fiction, visit
Inkandquillpress.com

Table of Contents

Beloved

Jan Abel

Beloved,

I can see where your annoyance with Sloane is coming from, but give her a little credit. She's alone in rank against two older brothers and two younger brothers. I more than understand. Please be kind to her, even if it leaves you her honorary "sister" for a few hours. Your sacrifice is noted and noble. Goodness knows if I could force Nora or Addie to go out on a hunt with me I would.

Speaking of, were you able to join your older brothers this year? I've always dreamed of being invited to the Glorious Donasian Hunt. All of those bears and boars and elk out in droves and ripe for the picking. It has to be amazing! Perhaps next year, I could accompany you?

I wait for the day that I can see your eyes under the redwood trees, and not simply in my imagination. Your prince,

Rowan

My prince,

The hunt is not nearly as exciting as you dream it is. It is days spent under the cold dampness of the coming winter, where you can't feel your fingers and you feast on little more than cold bread, jerky, and dried fruits. But if you insist on experiencing the, as you describe it, "glorious" hunt, then I suppose I can see what must be done for a foreign prince to take part.

I would much rather see the forests of Hvordi in the spring. Are the rhododendrons blossoming? Do those massive redwoods know to bloom in the spring, or does it take the whole season for the roots to tell the treetops that winter is done?

As for Sloane, I'm sure some may consider this "sacrifice" of mine as more of an education than anything. I've been told more than once that I'm far too boyish for my own good. Perhaps more people would be happy if I let Sloane succeed in this reeducation.

Let's meet under the stars then, even if it's only in our dreams.

Your beloved,

Ezra

I sit back from my desk, barely moving the quill off of the parchment in time before an excess glob of ink can stain the message.

I stare at the words below me: "your beloved." My mother would be thrilled—or maybe scandalized, who was to be sure these days—at the fact that I was *beloved.* Not just to anyone, but the second in line to the Hvordian throne.

Then again, she would also probably demand to read every correspondence between the two of us, both past and present. She would read about my distaste in the rigidity of royal life, even for those fourth in line. She would read about my complaints of how Rhett, Percival, and Solomon are treated versus myself and Sloane. Worst of all, she would read every occurrence where Rowan called *me* a prince.

I hadn't meant to lie to him. I had never even imagined the two of us would become pen pals, let alone lovers. And it wasn't like I had actually lied to the other man. I had simply...never corrected him.

A knock on the chamber door had me scurrying to close the rolling lid of my desk. I had barely sat back and smoothed the lap of my dress before Sloane walked in, a mischievous grin cracking her face in two.

"You will *never* believe what I overheard."

"Overheard, or eavesdropped?" I asked, raising an eyebrow as she flopped down on my bed, arms tossed out next to her. She waved one hand at me as if in dismissal.

"Shut up, you love gossip."

Rolling my eyes, I finally stood from my seat, sure she wasn't going to suddenly make a dash for my desk. I adored my older sister, I did, but she had to be the biggest gossip in Donas. Taking my perch next to her on the bed, I began to gently run my fingers through her long, thin hair. It was such a mirror of my own, I sometimes felt bad for hating it on myself. On Sloane, it was beautiful.

Her smile grew as she knew I had taken her bait.

"Father is looking at marriage candidates."

"Oh."

My stomach sank a bit. Already? Sure, Sloane may have been 19, but I wasn't ready yet. I wasn't ready for her to leave me. I wasn't ready to be the next one married off.

Rhett had married Eugenia three springs ago, and Mother was always going on and on about when she was going to be blessed with "tiny feet running amok."

Percival married Gwenivere only a few months after that.

It wasn't that I didn't like my sisters-in-law, but they weren't my oldest friend. They weren't my big sister—even if Sloane was only eleven months older.

If anything, Sloane's smile grew even more.

I could be happy for her. Even if the looming weight of 'next' swung above my head like a blade. My sister had dreamed of her wedding day since we were children running around the gardens. I couldn't burden her happiness.

"Father is looking for marriage candidates for *both* of us. Apparently, there have already been offers for our hands, and he appreciated having Rhett and Percy's weddings in such a close timespan."

It was then I forgot how to breathe.

***

I was sworn to secrecy by Sloane, but it was useless when a week later Father called us both to his study, Mother and a few of his advisors already waiting for us.

They had narrowed it down to five potential matches for Sloane. Three for me.

Option one: the eldest son to the Duke of Beahm. The Duke was a powerful ally amongst all of the dukes in Donas. Giving his son a royal wife would be a token of favor and recognition.

Option two: Colonel Witham. The youngest to ever reach the rank in the Donasian army. Injured in the line of duty, but proving an effective strategist and beloved leader to those still in training.

Option three: the nephew of the Queen of Leona. Not directly in the royal line, but well respected and close to those who *are*. Leona and Donas were on the brink of border skirmishes.

Mother preached about the importance of our roles in these marriages—these political alliances. We would serve our husbands as doting wives and confidants, with loyalty and understanding to our father's—and eventually eldest brother's—throne.

I quit listening the longer the meeting ran on.

It wasn't like I didn't know what my future would look like. We had been preparing for these days since we were children. Rhett and Percival—and to a lesser extent Solomon—on how to rule, fight, and lead. Sloane and I on how to be good wives, homemakers, and mothers.

I thought of Rowan. His imaginary promises of meeting me under the redwood trees. Not me—Princess Ezra Lillibet Amelia Autumnai; second daughter to the King of Donas, fourth in line for the Donasian throne—but *me*, his beloved prince.

I mourned a dream I hadn't realized I began to crave.

When we were dismissed, I barely remembered to duck my head to my father and mother before turning on my heel and marching for the door. I needed to get the hell out of here. I needed air that wasn't tainted by the perfumes of the castle. I needed to not be a princess, just for a moment. I only had moments left to be someone else as it was.

"Ez–"

Ignoring my sister, I made a break for it, not pausing even as she called out louder for me. I felt like a too big doll that Sloane or I would have once crammed into the dollhouse in our nursery. I couldn't breathe with the walls closing in around me. My bedroom door was thrown open as I stormed inside, barely remembering to close it before I was working free the buttons of my dress.

My shoulders burned from the way I wrenched them behind my back in an attempt to strip. As soon as enough were undone for me to slip the blasted thing over my head, I was throwing the garment onto the bed. Then the petticoats were kicked off, and the corset was unlaced at a speed I was sure my mother would call "improper." To hell with this, to hell with *all* of this. *I* was improper! I had an improper mind! And blast it if I could, I would live in impropriety just for the chance at being able to breathe freely.

The only time I could get away with trousers was when I went riding—and even then, I was at an age where Mother raised her eyebrow at my attire.

A simple tunic.

Trousers.

Vest.

Boots.

Cloak.

I was out the door before I even had the cloak clasped around my chest.

One of the joys—and trials—of growing up in a palace was that there were no secrets left in the place. I knew every crevice and every passageway with the same confidence I knew my own mind. It wasn't difficult to take less traveled paths out of the servants' entrance to the kitchens and down to the stables.

I gave the stable boy on duty a small nod and smile as he lurched upright upon realizing who was at the stalls. Waving off his offer to tack the horse, I moved with a practiced ease as I grabbed the saddle blanket. This was the same horse that I had learned to ride as a small girl. The older mare had actually taught all of the royal children how to ride. Although, both of the older boys had horses gifted to them when they had turned 18, and I *sincerely* doubted Sloane rode at all outside of official obligations.

There was a meadow just outside of the palace grounds. A brook flowed halfway through it that the mare took issue in stepping through. A large walnut tree sat off to the side, and in the springtime, this place was lovely. The tree was full of leaves that protected you from the afternoon sun. The grass grew tall and green with wildflowers dotting the landscape. But in the late autumn sun, everything was drying out, curling in on itself until winter was through. Poetic, I supposed.

Dismounting, I took a few jilted steps before collapsing under the walnut. Silent tears turned into hiccuping sobs as everything that had choked me since the minute Sloane had walked into my room one week ago came bubbling up.

Not for the first time, I imagined Rowan sitting next to me. I had never seen him, but we had described ourselves in letters, once.

I was shorter than either of my older brothers, and just barely taller than Sloane, who took after our mother in terms of height. My pin-straight hair was a light brown in the shadow and darker blond under the sun. I had worn glasses since I was a small child, and they were wide-rimmed, taking up over half of my face. My eyes were blue, my eyebrows narrow.

He had a mane of wavy black hair that came to the small of his back when held straight, and reached his shoulder blades when properly maintained. If it were a formal event, he would have it tamed into a single braid that would fall down the center of his back—the traditional style in Hvordi. His eyebrows were thick, and slightly bushy, casting his dark brown eyes into even more shadow. His skin was amber, and he had a dimple on his right cheek only.

He would wrap his strong arm around my shoulders and I would fit just under his cheek. He would tell me that everything was alright, and that I could succeed anywhere I decided to.

If anything, all it did was make me sob harder because he *wasn't* here, and I would be married off to some son of a duke who probably wouldn't appreciate his "wife" sending letters to a foreign man. There was no success here, only a hollow acceptance. I wondered briefly if this is how the hanged man felt on his way to the gallows. At some point, I exhausted myself, falling into a fitful sleep with my back propped against the rough bark of the tree.

In my sleep, I heard a laugh I only ever heard in my dreams.

***

"Princess Ezra? His Majesty has requested your company in his study at your earliest convenience," a servant said, quickly ducking his head as I looked over to him. Frowning, I stood, giving him a single nod before he was off on whatever task was next for him.

I had been penning a message for Rowan when the man had walked in, trying to figure out how to put into words the heartache I had felt over the past few weeks since hearing the news about my betrothal. How do you explain that your future has been narrowed down to who could present your family with the highest favor?

Shaking my head, I made my way out of my rooms, forcing myself not to wring my hands as I walked. A *good princess* does not wring her hands in worry where curious eyes could see.

My father was sat behind his massive desk as he bid me enter. The large window behind him provided enough light to fill the specific alcove that held his desk. His glasses had slipped down his nose to barely hang on the tip as his eyes met mine. He didn't smile at me, but he wasn't angry either. His face was painfully...neutral.

"There has been an offer for your hand, Ezra."

I forced my face to mirror his own.

"Oh?"

Who would it be? The duke? The colonel? Or the nephew?

Father held up an envelope that I hadn't noticed next to his hand. The familiar seal looked different in the light of my father's office, more ominous, more foreign.

"This was sent to me from the King of Hvordi, himself. Not a scribe on his behalf, not from an attendant. But from the king, himself. Talking about his interest in the *friend* of his eldest son, the second-in-line." He set down the envelope, never breaking eye contact. "I was unaware you were communicating with anyone, let alone outside of our borders." Again with that neutral tone. He wasn't upset, at least I didn't think he was. But he was cool, detached.

And how much did *Rowan's* father know? Did he call me a prince too? Did he know about our communication? It wasn't like our letters were a secret thing, but I guess I'd never actually asked.

"We were introduced by a mutual friend, they thought we were similar, and wanted us to meet," I answered carefully.

"Was your mutual friend the Hvoridan king, perhaps?" Father asked, raising an eyebrow. "He mentions in his letter how smitten his son is with you. He also says in no uncertain terms that there would be no one better for my child than his son." Father drops his gaze to retrieve a folded piece of paper, slowly opening the letter until he can find the line he was looking for. "The marriage would require you to move to Hvordi, and act as Hvordian royalty, though you won't have to denounce your Donasian citizenship. Should his eldest pass or abdicate and the prince should ascend, you would be named consort."

Father looked up at me again, calculating. "How does that sound to you?"

I swallowed. "I will do whatever you think is best, Father."

The improper sound of my father snorting broke the image of the impassive king I had been given since I walked into the room. When I met his eyes again, I found the father that would shovel eggs into his mouth and allow us to nap on his lap when we were tired children.

"Glad to hear you do listen to your mother, Ezra, but that's not what I asked. I asked: 'How does that sound to *you*?'"

Exhaling, I curved my shoulders inward, allowing a small smile to rise as I looked over to where Father had discarded the letter.

"It sounds," I paused, "Like a dream."

"A dream?"

"Rowan is one of the greatest people I've ever known," I said, straightening up. "He is kind, and caring, and he loves his nation and his sisters and his parents and poetry and hot bread he sneaks from the kitchens with fresh jam." I smile at the memory of the story, of him explaining how he brought some to his sisters and paid them off with extra butter so that they wouldn't snitch—specifically his older sister Eleanora. "I had wondered about him, when you announced I was eligible for marriage but I...didn't think it was an option."

Throughout my spiel, Father was silent, simply watching me as I spoke, his hands steepled in front of him. When it was clear I had nothing left to say he looked down for a moment to the folded letter again and then back to me.

"Then I suppose," he began, "I should send my own response to the king then," I watched as he picked up his pen, "and let him know that if he must take my daughter to the Hvordian court, then I at least demand a proper Donasian wedding. My youngest daughter deserves jewels and lace and silks, not just some quiet words under a few trees."

To hell with decorum or propriety. I threw myself at my father, wrapping my arms around his shoulders, even as he grunted in surprise before returning the hug.

It wasn't until later, as I laid down to rest that the high of the news receded, and I was left with a cold pit in my stomach.

When Rowan came to Donas, he would meet *her,* not his expected Beloved.

***

The Hvordian delegation arrived a month later with four carriages, five guards, two foot servants, two noblemen, and one prince. I watched them approach from the foot of the staircase in front of the grand entrance to the palace. My mother was to my left and my father to my right. Behind us, waited my siblings and a flurry of servants awaiting the group's arrival to usher their belongings to the suites we had set aside for them.

The corset I had on hugged my abdomen and pushed up my chest until I wasn't sure if I was going to choke on them or the bile steadily climbing up my throat. I had one too many petticoats on to the point it felt like I was dragging chains behind me. Perhaps it wasn't just the petticoats that had me like that.

When the carriages finally pulled to a stop in front of our waiting party, I only had time to swallow the bile and plaster on the smallest smile I could manage before the doors opened and a guard stepped out, bowing to the three of us before swiftly moving to the side.

"Allow me to present, His Royal Highness, Rowan Elijah Mountarbore, Crowned Prince of Hvordi."

He was more beautiful than he had described.

His hair was pulled back into a singular braid, his travel clothes loose but well-tailored. The wide smile he had was enough to make his eyes squint, and I could see the exact moment he took me in. Pin-straight hair pulled up and tight into an intricate bun that looked blond under the late afternoon sun. Large glasses that dwarfed the rest of my face. Strings of pearls and lace fabric covering every inch of my body in a show of propriety.

His gaze swept over mine, over my parents at either side, and took in my two older brothers behind me, arm-in-arm with their wives. He looked to where I knew Sloane stood, Solomon at her side. I knew the moment that our eyes met that he had gone over a mental tally of all of our letters. All of the times I had mentioned my sister and three brothers, and I saw the exact moment that the genuine smile that I had dreamed of every night turned to the polished royal look I mirrored.

As he approached, my mother discreetly nudged me, forcing me out in front of my parents in a reminder to bow, to curtsey. Swallowing, I lowered my eyes from his, keeping them firmly on his boots until he came to a stop. I moved like an actor on a stage, my eyes never leaving the dirt next to his foot.

"Prince Rowan," my father said, his deep voice smooth as heated caramel, "allow me to introduce you to my youngest daughter, Princess Ezra Lillibet Amelia

Autumnai." Standing back up, I kept my eyes down, swallowing again as the silence seemed to stretch into infinity. The sound of a throat clearing in front of me had my gaze darting up long enough to see Rowan holding out a hand to me, his smile strained. Unsure what else to do, I gave him my hand. His palm was worn but still soft, perfect for a nobleman. I tried not to think about how mine seemed to him as he bent down and gently pressed a kiss to my knuckles.

"A pleasure to meet you, *Princess*."

Somehow I didn't believe him.

***

It took six days into their visit for Rowan to corner me.

We had barely seen each other in general, let alone have the privacy to talk. But as the days passed I felt the tension building like a kettle coming to a boil. If I didn't remove it from the fire soon I have no idea who or what all I would burn. Every night was filled with extravagant dinners with Rowan and I sat across from one another but always surrounded by others. Every day was more "wedding preparation" and fittings and decisions that apparently were perfectly fine being made separately.

When there was a knock on my door then, that night, I should have known better.

There he stood, his white undershirt slightly untied at the juncture of his neck, and his vest gone—as was the braid.

Speechless, I gaped at him. I knew we needed to talk, had been trying to figure out how I could orchestrate something. But to come right to my door? In the family wing? If any of my siblings—God forbid my mother—had seen him–

Grabbing the front of his shirt, I yanked him inside, slamming the door shut as quietly as I could. When I turned back around I found him with his arms crossed, raking his gaze up and down my body.

My glasses had been discarded on my nightstand. My hair loose around my shoulders, tickling my neck and stretching down the white cotton nightdress I had changed into after dinner. Unconsciously, I crossed my arms over my chest, hunching forward as I dropped my eyes.

"Were you ever going to tell me?"

Silence.

A scoff. "So you were just going to let me live with a lie?"

"Rowan, I *never* lied to you." I hated the way my voice wavered.

"A lie by *omission* still counts! What? Did you think I wouldn't talk to you if you were a girl? Do you know how my people reacted when they saw *you* when they were expecting..."

"A prince?" I interrupted. Psyching up, I slowly raised my gaze until I met his.

I hated this. I had dreamed of us meeting for years, but never with that look of disgust on his face. The distrust.

"Rowan, I never lied to you," I repeated again, slower, my voice thick. "Well, I sort of, I, I'm not a prince but I..."

"You wished you were?" His voice was quieter, softer, something appraising this time as he looked me up and down.

"It's unheard of, I know, and my parents would never hear it, even if it was understandable. I promise, I can be a proper wife, if you'll give me the chan—"

"It's not—unheard of, I mean," Rowan jilted out. Taking a step closer, he raised his hand slowly, pushing back a strand of hair that had fallen in my face, cupping my cheek as his hand lowered.

"It's not common, but that doesn't mean it's not unheard of, at least, not in Hvordi. It's called *'satyrah,'* soul trapped. It means your soul was trapped in the wrong vessel." Tilting my head up I finally met his eyes as he cradled my face. His voice was indescribably soft, just as I had imagined it. "Are you *satyrah*, Beloved?"

I didn't realize I was crying, not until his thumb brushed underneath my eye. He was already slightly blurry without my glasses, and now it was even worse. It wasn't unheard of. It wasn't improper.

Slowly, Rowan's arms came down, wrapping around my shoulders and pulling me against his chest. He didn't say anything as I soaked the front of his shirt, standing there wordlessly as everything I had thought for years suddenly crumbled around me in ruins. It was *not* unheard of. It was *not* improper. It had a word!

With a laugh—perhaps a bit hysterical on my end—we broke apart, staying just within arms reach. As another thought came to me, my smile faded. My parents could never know, and that was fine. We were going to Hvordi anyway. But what about—

"Your father won't take issue with this? With me being a man? With being *satyrah*?"

"My father assumed you were a man to begin with. And I *told* you, being *satyrah* is uncommon, but it's not something to be ashamed of. Besides, father is planning to step down and pass the throne to Eleanora in a few years anyway." The look I must have given him hopefully asked what in the world the abdication had to do with anything. "Eleanora is *satyrah* too. Just...in the other direction." He cracked a smile that I felt myself begin to mimic. "If anything, Father will probably be happy he gets to have two sons again."

"Rowan, we need to keep this a secret," I said suddenly, reaching out to take his arm. "If my parents found out I...I don't know what they would do."

"Then let's go through with this," he said easily with a shrug. "All of the pageantry and the elegance and the bullshit that Donas apparently has to show off. And when it's over we'll go back to Hvordi," he stepped closer into my space again, tipping my face up until we slot together like two pieces of a puzzle, "we'll braid your hair back like mine." He ran his fingers through my blond hair. "We'll get you proper clothes for a prince." He pinched the fabric of my nightdress between his thumb and forefinger. "And we'll make our vows under the redwood trees." Our lips met, just a brush. When we pulled apart we were still close enough to breathe each other's air. "How does that sound, Beloved?"

It sounded perfect.

Opening the Birdcage

Velvet V. Nightengale

The roar of a thousand souls pulsed through the stone floor, the light of another clear day casting my husband's colosseum against an endless blue sky. I stare in its wake, tracing the distant lines of birds against the expanse, wishing any one of them could be me.

The scent of clay and man overpowers here, blood a secondary taste. The cavea are packed in all sections, citizens and nobles alike crammed in to see the show.

And what a show it promised to be.

"The war front has brought us new fighters again," the bemused voice of the emperor rose beside me, his hand touching my thigh. It was rough, the callouses of a warrior, although it had been long years since he'd himself seen battle.

"More each week," I replied absently, feeling the weight of the cuffs on my wrists with every brush of his skin on mine.

"Elveria," he spoke with intent, until I turned towards the man who'd married me, his dark eyes upon mine. "Do you still root for the wild man from the star fields?"

My heart hammered unevenly in my chest. I begged the skies that it did not show on my face. "It's hard not to, my lord," I answered with practiced care, "he always brings an entertaining fight."

The emperor is a man of hard lines and greying hair. His presence is a weight on one's chest, pressing the lungs of all who stand in his wake, and crushing the throats of all who displease him. I am in no mood to lose a battle of wits today, so I try to placate him with false words.

He studied me, a long, tense moment, until his sun-baked face cracked into a wide smile. "I see the holy lands have finally broken my pacifist wife," he gloats to the guards on his left, earning bemused chuckles. "In time, even the mages of the fields can appreciate the tastes of the empire."

The empire tastes like bile in my mouth and a binding spell on my wrists, but I don't say that out loud.

"Come now," Emperor Tirius leaned forward in his seat, waving for the fights to begin. The din of bloodthirst grows from the crowd, nearly drowning out his next words. "Let's see how your star field's champion fares against prisoners from the mountains."

There's a dark desire underwriting his words, a need for the reigning champion to fall. He's not the only one wishing for this, I knew. The holy empire did not want a hero of this colosseum unless it was one of their own.

They wanted to see him survive week after week, only to witness the final payoff when he was slain in combat, his life soaking into their clay.

I closed my hands together, watching for the gates to open from the prison below.

A new prisoner is shoved out first, a mountain of a man to match his home. He is shirtless, wearing loose linen pants and no further armor. One of his eyes is closed, an old scar from battle gluing it shut. He squinted into the sun with the other, his eyes circling the twenty foot walls surrounding the ring and the bodies on their feet for him. Food is thrown, jeers and slurs for his countrymen hurled just as harshly. He steps away from the onslaught, cursing the emperor and his men in a foreign tongue.

Barbarians, I thought of the men in the stands. *Snakes hiding beneath a veneer of society.*

Then, another form walked through the metal gate, and I could look nowhere else.

A fraction of the size of the other man, but no less impressive in build, the prisoner from the star fields stepped into the blinding daylight. His dark brown hair is growing long, but they cleaned him up for the fight—his face closely shaven, the cuts from last week healed over. He's broad in the chest, with the muscles of a fighter, particularly for the polearms our people favored before their fall. It made him leaner, unsuspectingly so.

Dust, sweat, and blood coat his bare torso, and he is all the more beautiful for it. He's always breathtaking when he fights, brought to life by brushing against death. His skin isn't as dark as it was when he arrived two months before, his tan fading from his time in a cell. But that look in his bright grey eyes—that sharp alertness about him—*that* had yet to dim.

I wondered what this country looked like through his eyes.

My fingers dig into the shackles at my wrists. They grow hot on the inside, fighting my magic that burns beneath my skin. It rises for him, a desperate swell of desire to lash out, to reach him, to feel his own—

Torture. I grab one of the shackles in my palm, my hand shaking with how tightly I hold it. Watching this man, this *stranger* week after week fight for his life, seeing all the men who fell to him, it was torture. Because he was down there facing death, and I was up here, wishing to run to him.

My time in this country had finally made me go mad, I realized. Years of my magic being repressed, of navigating this cut-throat court, of being on the beck and whim of a cruel emperor, I had finally snapped.

Because when he entered the ring, I no longer looked to the birds above.

I looked to *him*.

And I did not even know his name.

Jeers and condemnation rained down from the crowd, but he paid them no mind. He's silent, his eyes sizing up the man across from him, so large his shadow could eclipse a city.

My husband raises his hand again, a signal for the weapons to be thrown in. I hold my breath, two guards walking to the edge, an axe in one hand, a polearm in the other.

Then, just as he always did before a fight, the stranger's eyes flicked briefly to mine. Out of hundreds of eyes upon him, through the distance and the blinding sun, he finds me, and for a moment, I cannot breathe. I am lost in those eyes, paralyzed beneath that stare.

And then the weapons hit the ground, and he is the first to move, fast and sure on his bare feet.

I fear I will never move again, that I will never taste air in my lungs or life of my own.

The crowd screams for his death. I scream at myself to remain in my seat, to forgo these wild urges to climb over the wall, to drop all that distance and run to him, to touch him, to–

"I'll give him this much," my husband speaks to his guards mere moments later, when the champion fighter ducked under the swing of an axe and pierced the mountain's chest, hauling him up and over his body with a shout of effort to throw him far across the field, impossibly so. "He puts on one hell of a show."

My thundering heart stills in my chest at his next words.

"Next week, send in the general. I'm growing bored of this man from the star fields. It's time we show off the might of the empire to this prisoner, give my wife a *real* show."

***

It is the night before the next colosseum fight that I do something truly stupid. Blaming nearly a week without proper sleep, the heat of the stagnant summer nights, anything but the wire wrapped tight around my lungs since my husband's words, I acted.

Heart in my throat, my face hidden by a cloak far too heavy for the season, I slipped under cover of darkness from my husband's home and made for the colosseum. The city streets ignore me, just another traveller come to watch the show tomorrow. I kept to roads I knew to favor taverns and gambling dens, blending in with the unfamiliar faces and clothing styles of strangers.

Now I stood outside the imposing amphitheater, my hand brushing the white stone columns, my feet moving on their own. Ignoring the grand entrance I was usually pulled through I walked the distance around to the other side, where the steps to the underground dungeons lay.

Only one guard greeted me there, a relief. Two would have ended this foolish adventure far faster than I would have liked. The guard looked up, bored and tired at his overnight post, and before he could register my face I grabbed his, summoning within me every ounce of magic I could.

"*Sleep*," I suggested to him, the cuffs holding back far too much of my magic. Still, enough slipped out into him, and with his body so willing to obey he slumped against the wall, falling into a seated position, his breath heavy.

Sweat beaded my brow with the effort. Were it not for the binding spells woven into the metal cuffs my husband had bound me with such a suggestion would have been nothing. As it was, it had taken me years of wearing them, and thus my magic well naturally growing, to manage this much.

I slipped through the door unnoticed, latching it behind me.

I had never been down here. Not in all my time paraded around at the emperor's side had he deigned to visit the dungeons with me, and yet somehow a pull from deep within carried me forward. I forced magic to my hands again, a dim glow all I could manage as I navigated the winding halls, my eyes falling on sleeping prisoner after sleeping prisoner.

Far into the depths of the maze, in a cell set further from any other, I halted my steps. The light of my magic fell over the form of the star field champion, sitting near the bars of his cell, his head tilting up as if he'd been waiting for me.

I swallowed the tightness in my throat. Perhaps he had. Perhaps for more than just tonight. I step forward to the bars and he stands for me, his chest still bare, his height imposing, but not threatening. I stand just past the wall of his cage, finding that I had no idea what to say.

Still, my lips moved all on their own.

"Where have we met?"

"We haven't," he said, his voice low and rich with the accent of a home long since burned to the ground, "but I've been looking for you for a long time."

This close I can see he's no more than a few years older than I, perhaps thirty at the oldest. His body is covered in scars, many of them small, all from battles. He did not sing with the magic of our people, but he wore our colors, same as mine. The tan skin. The dark brown hair, my own long yet pinned behind my head. The light eyes.

I gripped the bars of his cell, the light still playing off my hands. "I know you," I whispered, digging into his eyes with my own for answers unforthcoming. "Yet, we've never met. This mystery endlessly haunts me. I can't sleep, I can barely eat. I feel like I'm going mad."

I hadn't meant to admit that to him. I hadn't... honestly, I hadn't known *what* I had meant to say. Why I had come down here. How I had made my way to him as if summoned when no magic called to me.

None that I knew, anyway.

"Tell me your name," I demanded of him, but the words came out with no authority. Only quiet fear.

Those grey eyes, so much my own, took me in and shone with understanding I did not ask him to give. "Lucan," he answered me, "Lucan of the Star Fields."

"Lucan," I whispered aloud, the name brushing my senses like a finger down my spine. It was a name I had never heard, yet all at once knew, just as I did him.

"And yours?" He asked, leaning forward against the bars with his forearm above his head.

"Elveria, wife to Lord and Emperor Denacus," I answered without thought, the title as worn on my tongue as bowed steps from a thousand years of use.

"Wife," Lucan asked, "or captive?"

The bands on my wrist weighed heavy. I closed my hand across one, as if to protect it from the allegation drenched in truth. "Is there any difference in this world?" I couldn't help but ask, the words as bitter as ash. "In this country? The whims of the emperor are law, and all who go against it are as good as dead. He claimed me as his wife, a prize for winning, so his wife I am."

I close my eyes to the memories, my city burning around me, the man on horseback standing over me, my magic spent and useless. The day we lost. The day I was taken, barely a woman. The night I was bound, and wed, and forced to parade at his side, a trophy of war.

Lucan's hands shot through the bars, grabbing me above my wrists and pushing my sleeves back with force. I gasped from it, and yet his grip was only firm, never painful.

"To bind your reach to magic is worse than death," Lucan snarled, but his anger wasn't directed towards me. "That man has taken something beautiful from this world and wrapped it in iron to match his jewelry of the day."

"Lucan," I begged, but he went on.

"He holds you like a possession, an object, yet he knows nothing of what you are, *who* you are. *That* is a crime where death is a forgiving punishment."

"You don't know me either," I was quick to argue, tugging my wrists away and stepping back.

"I do," he insisted, placing a closed fist on his chest, his eyes intense. "In here, just as you do me. We are soul bound, through this life and many, Elvie. You know it just as I."

Elvie. No one had called me that in a long, long time. Nicknames required endearment, and no one had been dear to me since the death of everyone I had known. Fear thundered through my body, fear at his words, worse than heresy, fear at his strength, though he had not hurt me, and worst of all...

Fear that he was right. That the man locked away before me was the other half of my soul, a myth as old as magic, a tale as impossible as stopping time.

"No," I said, desperately shaking my head and taking another step back. "No, we're not."

Pain, so sudden it cracked something within me, too, flooded his eyes. "Elvie," Lucan started, reaching for me.

"No," I shook my head again, "it's a trick, this... familiarity. A magic I do not know."

You'll give me hope that there's something more for me in the world. That there's something worth dying for to escape this place.

Tears flowed freely as I looked upon him again. "Tomorrow, he means to have you killed," I confessed, my chest shattering with the admission. "He's setting you to fight his general, a man who rode alongside him when they slaughtered our home. He's experienced against our fighting styles, has never lost a fight, and even if he falls..."

The archers. I'd seen my husband use them once, when a man thought to send a spear barreling towards the emperor instead of his opponent. The fate of those who do not play the game.

Lucan's eyes harden with determination, not the least bit shaken by the knowledge. "Elvie," he said, "I have felt your song for most of my life, calling to me like a far away bird, whispered on winds and across lands. It pulled my body towards you across time and distance, through wars and worse, to find you. We are soul bonded, a magic so old and deep it transcends the beginning of the world, and nothing, not even the threat of death, could keep me from coming for you." He searched my eyes for something I was afraid I did not have to give. "I will always come for you, across the heavens or earth, just as you have tonight for me. I do not fear death, only that I would never get to speak to you before it found me."

"I cannot save you," I whisper to the floor, looking away from him. "I am useless, untethered from my magic. You have come all this way for nothing."

"We both knew you could not free me tonight," he said softly, acceptance in his tone. "But tell me, my fallen star, *why* did you come to me tonight?"

Why indeed. Silence stretched between us, words again failing me. He waited, giving me precious time he did not have. Then, once more, I spoke without thought, right from the heart.

"I need you," I whispered, tears falling freely down my cheeks. "I need you, and I don't know how, or why, but the pull has driven me to fight myself for weeks, to hold myself back every time you were in the ring from climbing the wall and racing to you, and now that you're here in front of me, you're so far away, and I don't know what to even ask of you, or *what* I can ask of you–"

Lucan's hands are rough on my face, his knowing eyes filling my vision.

"When I said I would always come for you, I meant it in *every* sense of the word, my fallen star."

My chest burned white hot, threatening to scald me from the inside out. His touch is no better, setting my skin aflame. My magic roars within me, crashing against my bonds, pushing outwards, struggling to break free.

At his words, everything I am fights to unleash from this gilded cage I've put myself in. My place in the world, my titles as consort, as wife, it all ignites and turns to cinder then ash before him.

I am undone.

I am everything I've tried to convince myself I could never be again.

I press my cheeks against the bars, painfully so, and capture his lips in mine. Hunger throws me off the cliff, and he is ready to catch my fall. His mouth moves with me, heedless of the cold steel between us.

A whine escapes my lips, so unbefitting of my station. I want more. I need it, but the cell holding him keeps me achingly at bay. Close enough to touch him, to breathe him in and beg for his body against mine, but separated by literal bars heedless of my need.

Our kiss is desperate, unwinding weeks of tension I'd held barely at bay. When I pull back to breathe it is with a gasp, his eyes finding mine, and we both know it's not enough.

Nothing this man could ever give me would be enough. Not until I had him wholly.

He tears my cloak away, the fabric coming apart at the clasp. I gasp again at the sensation, violent and quick, and at the cold air that rushes in to greet me. Beneath it I am wearing a light summer dress, my thighs exposed, the fabric barely covering my shoulders.

His eyes roam me in hunger, taking in my breasts, my hips, finally available to him up close. I feel utterly exposed to him, and all it serves to do is raise my excitement.

"Beautiful," he says, his voice a mix of wanton lust and a hunger that matches my own.

"Come here," he commands, reaching through the bars for me again. I step eagerly forward, drunk on his low, husky tone. His hand cups the back of my head, fingers entwining in my loose hair, and I let myself be pulled in for another kiss, longer and more desperate than the first. The bars press between our cheeks, cold and unyielding, but I don't care. Everywhere he touches me is alive, a heat that burns away the metal chill.

His other hand guides mine to the front of his pants and a shock runs through me at the feel of him, hard and desperate for me. Every sensation is dual, both exploratory and new, yet as familiar to me as my own body. In this life we are strangers, but deep within us, something untouchable and older than time, we are bound together.

My body aches for him, and I know he feels the same. The rational mind is overridden by something greater than ourselves, and I need to be close to him, in any way I can.

I am his, and he is mine. My magic sings for him beneath my skin.

"Turn for me, my fallen star," he breathes in the space between us, his voice low, his eyes as lost as mine. I obey him, turning around in his arms until he grabs my hips, pulling me back flush with the bars. I gasped, but not from pain. I can feel him pressing against me, hard heat pushing against fabric between us.

"Please," I begged him, because there were not enough words in any language to describe what I needed.

Lucan understood, as I knew in my soul he would. His hands pushed my dress above my hips, his fingers finding my core and sliding in with no resistance. He moves within me as if he knows me, his fingers curling to the perfect spot on the first try.

I cover my mouth, muffling the sound he elicits. We are separated from the other cells by distance, but that distance was only a short, empty hall.

"Elvie," he breathes, pulling his fingers from me only to push down his trousers and press against my entrance once more, "even if this is all I have of you, even if I face my death tomorrow, know that I will die a fulfilled man."

Tears threaten at his bittersweet words once more, because this will never be enough. Now that I've touched him, tasted him, held his skin against mine, I know that nothing will ever be enough.

I know that I will find this man across time and lives, just as I have tonight.

He slides into me, his size stretching me, more and more entering me, his hands holding my hips as far back against the bars as he can. I arch my back for him, standing on tiptoes hoping to give him better reach. He cannot seat himself fully within me, but even this was more than I could take, my pleasure peaking, my body cumming simply from the sensation of him within me.

"Lucan," I breathe his name like a prayer, sparks burning my wrist from the cuffs when my magic burst forth, unbidden.

"Elvie," he moans for me, his hands coming to wrap around my stomach, my sternum, pulling me upright and holding me everywhere he can. His motions are desperate, rushed, both of us aware faintly that we had so little time. It was so much more than desire pulling us together, so much more than lust.

I close my eyes to the hallway, imagine myself in a place I hadn't thought of in so long, both of us together beneath the wide open night sky back home, the silvery grass shining with a thousand dots of stars far above.

I feel my pleasure mounting again, rise with the tide once more, feel him press as much of his forehead as he can in my hair, our bodies threatening to melt through the prison between us.

"Lucan," I called back, "I'm..."

"With me," he whispered, "once and for always, my fallen star."

I keep my eyes closed, blue sparks of light beyond them like the thousand stars in my mind. I feel myself ascending, again and again, higher and higher, until with one final thrust he binds us both, filling me, filling my heart.

My magic burst forth with a force greater than it ever had, crashing against the shackles with a roar through my bones, and with burning worse than any fire I'd ever felt I opened my eyes to see the cuffs glowing a bright blue, cracking at the onslaught until...

Until they both shattered, raining from my wrists with metallic shards upon the floor.

Lucan doesn't release me as my body falls forward, holding me upright while I learn to breathe for the first time in years, still connected at the hips. My breaths come out as loud gasps, my magic rushing back to me and settling within me, a vibrant, unburdened light.

"My cuffs," I breathed, staring at my wrists in awe, deep burn marks wrapping around them where they'd laid.

"You overwhelmed them," Lucan guessed, his words filled with pride and awe. I turned to him, sliding forth until we disconnected and I could see him in full. The room had been so dark before, now it glowed in my mind where my magic reached out and touched it, spilling from me once again.

I swallowed, still in shock, my heart hammering in my chest. He looked upon me with love in his eyes, so foreign a stare I could nearly cry.

"You will not die tomorrow," I breathed, reaching for the lock. With a whisper of will it shattered in my hands, the power of a true sorceress of the star fields returned at last. "Not when I have just found you."

He fixed his pants, coming through the open door to grab me and pull me into a long, deep kiss. My body sang where he touched me, wrapping my arms around him and enjoying every delicious point of contact.

He pulled back before my desires would pull him against the nearest wall, fighting his own urges. "Then we run," he said, grinning so brilliantly for me. All for me.

I nodded. "Then we run."

***

Lucan helped me up on the horse, a polearm strapped across his back. Behind us the colosseum burned a bright blue, the streets overrun with panic and war prisoners loosed into the madness of a city who'd taken them for their sick games.

"The empire will never stop hunting us," I warned, fear coating my bones. I tugged my cloak tighter, my chest tightening with the thought of losing this man, this other half of myself so soon after finding him. He settled my back against his chest, taking the reins.

His eyes shine bright with moonlight, his smile wide and flashing. He is breathtaking, brought to life as always by brushing against death, an eternal dance.

"Then I will treasure every moment we have," he answers my fears, "and fight for every moment more."

"They will find us someday, no matter where we go."

"Then I will find you again in the stars," he lowers his voice, cupping my face to press our lips together in a long, tantalizing kiss we did not have time for. Still I let myself fall into it, into that foreign feeling of *home*.

"I will always come for you," he breathed, "my fallen star."

The horse carried us fast and far, the city a burning collection of lights far behind us, a vast sky before. Pressing my chest to his back I closed my eyes, breathed in the scent of him, felt the wind of the world surrounding us, magic and alive, and wondered if this was how birds felt to fly.

In All The Realm

Jenessa J. Lumberry

"What can I get you, miss?" The tavern keeper asked, eyes focused on his latest patron. A bard played an upbeat tune in the corner as he cleaned a glass upon her approach. Other customers raised their eyes from their meals and hushed conversations, curiosity thick in the air.

The young woman groaned in drunken exasperation as she fell into the seat across from him, blonde hair mussed, grey eyes puffy from crying and the smell of wine already on her breath. These were all something the tavern keeper knew very well as promising signs of entertainment. She was interesting to look at. The tavern keeper couldn't put his finger on it, but while she was beautiful there was a roughness to her. Her ashen blonde hair was thick and pulled back haphazardly with a ribbon. She was of average height and build, but he could assume easily from how she moved that she had at least some muscle and curves under her riding clothes.

The bartender set the glass aside and propped his elbows on the aged wood, settling his chin into his hands with a practiced grin.

"Come now, miss, tell the old bartender what weighs upon your soul?" His voice was playful, his smile melting into something more impish. The man truly was a sucker for good gossip and this young lady looked like she had a plethora of it.

"Gods," she moaned, "get me a drink first, please?" Her voice was rich with an accent, the words rolling off her tongue with decadence. Her gray eyes softened from winter cold steel, to something more approachable. She was clearly not from around here and didn't seem to notice the attention she garnered from the room.

The tavern keeper chuckled, pouring a shimmering pink liquid for the pitiful creature before him.

"Why are men all the same?" She started, taking the glass and inspecting it, deciding it would do.

She sighed contentedly when the honeyed wine touched her tongue. The one before her was...cute. Almost too plain really, boring to look at. Hells, the man didn't even have any noticeable scars, just smooth, sun tanned skin. He couldn't have been more than a few years older than her, with shoulder-length brown hair and soft amber-brown eyes.

"Love troubles I take it?" The bartender laughed, the mischievous gleam she kept catching in their depths sparking in his eyes. "You poor thing, you look in need of a shoulder to cry on, Miss...?"

She sniffled and set the glass down, wiping her mouth with the back of her sleeve. "Judeah."

The tavern keeps eyes glinted, "Just Judeah?"

She hiccuped. "Asterin"

"Judeah Asterin." He said her name carefully, as though playing with how the words felt in his mouth. "Well, you can call me Ambrose. Now," he pushed his brown hair back and out of his face, "something must have happened to lead you to my tavern with such bitter words. Come," Ambrose said, "tell me all about this man."

"Men!" She practically wailed.

Ambrose cooed sympathetically, patting her hand with barely hidden anticipation. "Let it all out."

"Are you sure?" Judeah asked, cheeks going rosy as fresh alcohol began to flood her senses.

He nodded. "Absolutely, listening to the tales of travelers is all part of my job."

Judeah hesitated for a moment more. "Well...if you insist," she started.

Judeah looked down at her glass, voice hesitant. "Have you ever spurned the heart of someone with power?"

Ambrose gave her a curious look, his interest piqued. He hadn't heard a truly enticing tale of love gone wrong in quite some time. His eyes noted the faintest scar at the corner of her mouth, one he found himself wanting to touch.

"Have you?"

Judeah drained the other half of her glass, a fire entering her eyes, giving them the illusion of heated steel straight from the hottest forge. "I have. Gideon Sol Morgenson of Velaire."

Now that name gave Ambrose pause. He'd heard it plenty of times from his patrons. "The famous hero?" He inquired, eyebrows raised.

She laughed bitterly. "The very same. I was young and naïve to the ways of men back then, and he was so kind, nothing like what you would expect from someone who can boast about being the hero of all the realm! You expect some pompous prick who bought the title, but he was every inch what a legendary hero should be." Judeah trailed off, as if overtaken by a memory. "He swept his way into my life with such force that my world absolutely revolved around him."

Ambrose refilled her glass, and pushed it back to her. "He sounds like the perfect man," he supplied, raising an eyebrow. "So what changed? What could such a man have done to earn your ire?"

Judeah shifted in her seat, eyes flicking downward, her fingers tracing a knot in the wooden bartop. She looked like a woman that would normally present herself as confident and put together, but speaking of Gideon seemed to drain that from her, she looked like a lost, kicked puppy.

"Nothing at first, Gideon was a fantastic man, partner...lover. My family was thrilled with the match."

Ambrose tried to meet her eyes. "How long were you with Gideon?"

"Three years," she replied perhaps a bit too quickly, looking up to meet his gaze. "The first year was bliss. Damnit, even the sex was phenomenal! We spent days and nights attached at the hip. Every little second with him felt special. For the first time in my life I felt like I meant something to someone. "

A few of the patrons glanced their way when her voice rang out a touch too loud, and Ambrose shot them a warning look to mind their own business. He would not have any of these idiots ruining his entertainment. His few remaining patrons knew better than to meddle after that look and shifted their attention towards anything but the two at the bar.

Ambrose reached out and touched her arm, nodding in encouragement. "You were saying?"

Judeah tried and failed not to look embarrassed by her own outburst. "But in the second year, things got... complicated. Gideon didn't become the hero of all the realm by staying in one place, and he took his title very seriously. Any call to action, and he was off in the blink of an eye. Skirmishes, turf wars, monsters, even a committed rival! I might as well have been alone. I tried my best to be understanding while still making my dissatisfaction known, and Gideon eventually attempted to remedy things by proposing."

"And you said no?" Ambrose asked.

"Worse, I said yes." She grimaced, "I thought we were turning things around, getting back to the lovers we were in the beginning, and I was twenty-three at that point, practically a spinster!"

"Not a spinster!" Ambrose covered his mouth in mock horror, earning him a steely glare.

Judeah flipped him a wayward middle finger, earning a chuckle and a wink from the tavern keeper. She pouted and looked away.

He sighed, waving a hand. "I'm only teasing, don't take it to heart. I understand that the expectations of young ladies nowadays are immense." Ambrose's face shifted, expression thoughtful. "Please, continue."

Judeah huffed but began her tale again. "I started wedding planning, but after a while, I realized nothing would ever change. No matter how much Gideon wanted to give me the life he promised, the long absences never ceased, nothing changed. I would always come second to his duties no matter how much I loved him."

The tavern around them had quieted considerably, the room was now merely dotted with a few patrons, while the bard in the corner lazily plucked at the strings of his lute, playing something soft and discordant. Ambrose hardly cared though, didn't even notice Judeah's glass that he had been neglecting. He was riveted, feeling the true tension of this tale just a breath away.

Judeah exhaled. "Still, I tried to make the most of a bad situation. Until something happened that changed everything."

Ambrose purred, taking her glass and refilling it, "Go on."

She took the glass with a nod of thanks, but did not bring it to her lips. "Gideon had been gone for quite some time. I hadn't seen, let alone heard from him in months. Wedding plans had long since become escape plans. I was using all that time alone plotting a way to leave without losing my livelihood and self respect. When suddenly the estate Gideon had been housing me in was raided by none other than his rival, Sir August Nightstorm."

Yet another name Ambrose had heard whispered in his tavern many times before.

"The infamous shadow sorcerer?" He asked, beginning to suspect where this was going.

"The one and only. He was seeking out Gideon to challenge him, but outside of an empty keep, there was only me."

"What happened?"

"He surprised me. I was ready to fight him off, for all the good that would do, but he looked at me with such pity." Her face twisted, something between sadness and anger in her eyes. "He could see how I'd been left by Gideon to toil on my own, lonely and frustrated. Hells, he even apologized to me for pulling my lover away. I told him not to pity me, not to even dare it. That I was leaving before long and Gideon had no one to blame but himself. So he offered me a deal."

This made Ambrose take pause, his eyes almost flashing.

"A deal?"

"A deal that he would take me wherever I wanted and help me get a new start, if I was willing to play along and let Gideon think he had kidnapped me. I was so angry at Gideon for leaving me alone for so long that I agreed." She let out a breath, and looked up at Ambrose with a tired smile. "Anything was better than being stuck like a damsel in a tower."

"And I take it Gideon did not take this well at all?" Ambrose asked.

Judeah laughed bitterly. "No. Oh, he searched for me for a time, but then after a while the excuses started. Bigger disasters to take on, villagers who were weak and helpless without him when I was strong and could manage." She bit her lip, hard enough that it nearly bled. "As soon as I heard that, I knew I'd made the right decision. Gideon had shown me just how little I mattered to him. It didn't take long after that for me to let myself notice how charming August was. He was fun, and honestly quite attractive in that broody kind of way."

Ambrose smiled knowingly. "The best villains always are." For a moment he, too, looked lost in a memory.

Judeah nodded, "And it's not as if he were a horrendous person, either. He just did what he wanted. He made efforts to not let people get hurt and I respected that."

"So, how long did it take for the bad boy appeal to fade?" Ambrose smirked.

Judeah shrugged, looking embarrassed. "You're going to make fun of me if I tell you," she mumbled, another drunken little hiccup escaping with the words.

Ambrose chuckled. "I give my word that I will not laugh at you, no matter what."

He watched Judeah chew the inside of her cheek, mulling over whether she believed him. Finally she sighed, relenting.

"The man was far too obsessed with Gideon." She grumbled, a sour look on her face.

To Ambrose's credit he did not laugh. But, by the gods, did he want to.

Instead, he cleared his throat and looked away from the girl's scrutinizing gaze that promised violence at even the barest hint of a chortle.

"See? I didn't laugh." He insisted, still not meeting her gaze while he refilled her glass. "Please, do go on."

Her narrowed eyes stayed on him, but she did.

"As I was saying...he was obsessed. Every activity we did, every conversation we had, hell even the pillow talk always managed to loop back to Gideon! Towards the end I even put a knife to his throat and swore if he so much as breathed Gideon's name one more time I would cut him from nose to navel." She smacked her palms on the bartop, eyes going molten again. "He just laughed and said I was being ridiculous, and used his magic to disarm me. It was humiliating. When I didn't calm down he locked me in an actual tower!"

Ambrose nearly winced at the venom in her voice. The barely tethered wrath in her eyes compelled him to lean closer, hanging onto every word.

"Can you believe that?" She rolled her eyes before taking the last swig of her drink. "The man that claimed to love me and seemingly saved me from what I had seen as a gilded cage, was now locking me away. I was not having it. Not again."

"Thus, all men are the same." Ambrose surmised, amused.

Judeah continued on as if she didn't hear him. "When one of his servants brought me my first meal in that cell, I didn't hesitate. I pushed through, taking his keys and gathered what I could of my things, and a few of August's to sell later. Maybe August thought since I never got around to leaving Gideon, I would simply do the same with him. But he underestimated me, I will never again sit idly

by and twiddle my thumbs waiting for some man. I left."
That fire in her eyes seemed to dim, and she settled back
down onto her seat, shoulders slumping. "Now both of
those idiots are looking for me, and I refuse to go back to
either of them. I will no longer be caged."

Ambrose was quiet. Mulling over the end of her
story. "So," he asked, "where will you go now? What will
you do if they catch you?"

She stared into her glass solemnly, "I...I had
considered chartering a ship to stay with my cousins on the
coast." She took a deep breath before looking back to
Ambrose. Her chest ached at the idea of running away with
her tail tucked between her legs.

"I've never been on my own before, and I don't wish
to burden my family with this. My loved ones deserve
peace...I do not wish for peace. I am tired of trying to
pretend to be someone I'm not."

A slow grin began to creep across Ambrose's face.
He reached out, touching her arm, his hand warm.

"What if I could help you?"

Judea snorted at the question, voice sarcastic as she
swirled the liquid in her cup, rotating the glass
methodically. "How? Are you going to offer me a job? I
suppose they would never expect to find me working as a
tavern wench." she said, her smile tight with distaste.

Ambrose threw his head back and laughed. It was
an odd sound, melodious and beautiful with an undertone

of something more. It made Judeah pause and take her first good look at the man, breaking from her melancholic reverie.

Ambrose was handsome for sure, but there was something off about him now that he had her full attention.

She hadn't noticed it in her intoxicated haze when she first wandered in but something was off about the tavern keeper. She wasn't scared of him, but she was certainly uneasy now.

"Not exactly," Ambrose finally replied, "but seeing your penchant for deals, I thought I might offer you one of my own."

"...What kind of deal?" She asked slowly, suspicion laced through her words.

Ambrose leaned forward and steepled his fingers. "Well, you've already given me so much it's only fair I give you something in return," he crooned.

"But I haven't given you anything?" She said in confusion, her back straightening. Something about his eyes and the way with which he spoke now made her feel like prey caught in a snare.

Ambrose tilted his head. "No need to be so wary dear, it's far too late for that."

It was then that Judeah finally noticed it. The absolute silence. The sounds of the busy tavern were absent and when she glanced behind her she realized that all the patrons, the performing bard in the corner, everyone, was gone. It was just her, and Ambrose, and the eerie stillness.

Judeah stumbled off of her stool, knees wobbly from the effects of too many drinks. "Who are you?" She whispered, a hand fumbling for the knife on her belt, "What are you?"

Ambrose chuckled. "Fret not child, I mean you no harm. I cannot lie to you or your kind."

Her eyes widened as understanding dawned on her. This man—no, this creature—was one of the faire folk. Creatures that far outlived humans, primarily dwelling in lands beyond the veil of this plane of existence. Most of the fae that resided in the human lands were low-powered tricksters that took delight in pranks and unbalanced deals. Most.

The fae, for one reason or another, couldn't lie to humans. They relied heavily on speaking in riddles and rhymes. It was very uncommon, but not unheard of, for higher fae to make their way through the veil, and to disguise themselves as humans for a bit of fun.

Only now did she realize that not only was Ambrose fae, but if he had concealed his fae identity so seamlessly that she couldn't tell him apart from a human person, he must be a high fae of some kind.

Ice ran through her veins until she stood paralyzed by this knowledge. He had said she'd already given him something. Fuck...what had she given him? Judeah tried to rack her brain as she glanced around for an escape.

Ambrose gave a deep sigh and rolled his eyes, eyes that had begun to glow a warm gold like a sunset.

"As I said child, I will not hurt you. Now," He said, beckoning her back to the stool with a lazy wave of his hand" sit."

When she didn't move his eyes narrowed.

"Sit, Judeah Asterin."

Her name. She had given this thing her name, the one thing you were never to do when it came to the fae. Judeah felt her legs move of their own accord as she made her way back to her seat and sat, her frame stiff with tension.

"Humans, always so touchy," He sighed in exasperation, his form shimmering, as if he were only barely holding together the threads of the glamour he had worn all night. His brown shoulder length hair turned to something longer and the color of rust, finer facial features showing through the facade.

"What do you want?" She demanded.

"As I said, you've already given me much tonight. Your name, and a very entertaining story. So I shall give you two things in kind." He held up one finger over his lips as if he were about to tell her a secret, "The first and most important; for your name, I will grant you my protection... so long as you stay within my sight, of course."

Anger and despair filled her eyes. "You mean be your pet? I tell you I no longer wish to be caged and that's exactly what you intend to do to me yourself!"

"I'll have you know I take excellent care of my pets." Ambrose huffed, looking at her in mock offense, "There will be no gilded cage for you though, of that you have my word. You may leave anytime you please, but outside of my protection and care...I cannot promise your safety."

Judeah swallowed hard. "And the second thing?"

"For keeping me entertained for the night, I owe you a night of entertainment."

She paused, eyes wary but curious "What does that entail?"

He leaned forward to whisper in her ear, voice low and husky. "I suppose it depends on what you find entertaining."

She felt her cheeks heat.

Ambrose laughed that beautiful dark laugh again, leaning back with a feline grin. "Carnal pleasures are certainly on the table."

"I never said–" she sputtered.

"No, but your eyes did. You have a very expressive face," he added, his fingers tracing down her cheek to take her chin. His touch was soft and warm.

Judeah sucked in a breath and tried to look away from him.

Ambrose's expression became playful. "It's not a sin to yearn for pleasure. Your kind is so determined to deny yourselves such things, but I have no such shame. Feeding your lust would be a more than acceptable way to repay you for tonight's fun."

She considered everything before her. Ambrose couldn't lie to her, that much she knew. The fae were tricky, sure, but right now he was speaking plainly, not in riddles like her parents and maids had always warned her of when speaking of the faire folk.

Judeah did not want to trust anyone—let alone some high fae bartender—with her protection.

She also didn't really want to be alone, especially now that she was running from both Gideon and August. And, well, what else would she do? She had been wandering aimlessly for about a month now, had no real plan, and was running out of money fast. And despite this man being of the fae, she had strangely felt more care and compassion from him then from people who had claimed to passionately love her. She almost felt like she was betraying herself by feeling safe with him...but what else was she to do?

"Ok," she whispered.

"Come again?" The fae man coaxed, he needed unwavering agreement.

She looked up, eyes meeting his. "Your deal, and your terms...I accept. Both your protection, and...and the entertainment." Her cheeks reddened and she nearly faltered on those last words.

Ambrose hummed in glee and held his free hand out between them.

Judeah took it, expecting him to shake on it, but instead he pulled her close and kissed her. His lips tasted of honey, fresh spring grass, and something floral and dark. There was also a strange heat that seeped into her from every point of contact with the fae male. Tendrils of sunlight filled her at his touch, delicious and dizzying.

"What are you doing?" She said, pulling away clumsily, breath heavy and eyes wide.

"Sealing it with a kiss." He chuckled, his own breath labored.

The sound of the heavy front door swinging shut startled her back into reality. They were back in the tavern as it had been before he had revealed himself to her. The smattering of patrons had further dwindled, and the bard now fast asleep with his lute in his lap.

Judeah swayed a bit as she tried to create space between them. She felt strong arms around her, finding Ambrose's human face hovering above her, that impish grin back in place.

"Gus," he called to another man on the other side of the room, "my shift is done and I'm going to show my friend here to her quarters. She's quite tired."

When Gus nodded and made his way behind the bar Judeah swore she could see horns coming out of his head, just out of the corner of her eyes. Ambrose scooped her up with ease, as if she weighed no more than a child and not a fully-grown woman in a heavy cloak and riding clothes. She didn't complain, though.

She was tired and it felt nice to lean on someone like this, and to let them take care of her, even for just a moment.

He carried her up a set of stairs and into the upper floors of the inn. Now that they were alone again, she felt his lips come back down to press onto hers.

"The night is still young. And I think you've more than earned your reward." He whispered, voice pleasantly husky. It sent a shiver of longing up her spine.

Ambrose opened a door at the end of the hall. The bit of moonlight filtering through the curtains made it possible for her to make out a large bed in the room, which he unceremoniously tossed her onto.

"Hey!" She yelped in surprise when she landed heavily.

Ambrose stood at the foot of the bed looking down at her with eyes that glowed once more. "Undress. Unless you wish for me to do it for you."

She bit her lip and looked at him, his form shimmering again as if he was barely holding onto the glamour on his skin. She wanted this. It had been so long since she had seen anyone look at her so intensely. Even if she didn't quite understand why Ambrose eyed her like that, she couldn't deny how much her body responded to him and the command, so she obeyed.

He undressed as well. In the darkness she could see more of his true fae form, his pale body lean muscled and movements elegant, he had many scars and she was almost certain she could make out the beginnings of a tattoo that curved around his sides from his back.

In the soft light, both of them bare and drinking each other in, she felt her heart race at the way those glowing eyes took in every curve of her body. The desire in his eyes was overwhelming and heating her at her very core.

"Who knows, perhaps after tonight you will give me one more thing," he said, moving until he was on top of her, his body warm and inviting against her bare skin.

"Like what?" She whispered.

He took his time, trailing kisses and soft bites up her stomach and breasts, then shoulder and neck until his lips met her ear. "Your heart."

Smoke and Fire

Anika Drew

Norse mythology tells us that smoke and fire represent the powerful forces of nature. Likewise, as symbols of wisdom, memory, and transformation, crows are said to carry with them messages of the divine and represent creation and knowledge.

She felt his touch, tendrils of smoke, caressing her thighs. It smothered her fears, choked her with tenderness and desire.

As the heat spread out from her core, Madeline Ravenswood focused on her breathing. *Slow down,* she told herself, *breath in 2, 3, 4, hold 2, 3, 4, and release.* The mantra worked for a minute, maybe less, before her body took back over and began the climb to her first orgasm.

"I...can't ..." she groaned.

"Yes, you can," the man above her whispered in her ear. His hands slid up her body to her shoulders, then moved to her back as his mouth worked its way from her belly button to her breasts.

"I want you to let go. I want you to let me in. Let me hear you—see you—tell me what you want, what you need," he murmured against her heated flesh.

Making his way back down her body, his voice disappeared between her thighs and her mind escaped at the same time.

Fantasy blended with reality and she was soaring high above, tearing through clouds as the thunderstorm broke. Her body no longer attached to her mind, she let loose with a cry of pleasure, not hearing his moan of satisfaction.

Eyes shut firmly, she felt, rather than saw, the rain begin. Flashes of lightning illuminated them both as other eyes watched. Pinpoints of light caught in the eyes of the crows high above them in the trees. Heads cocked to one side or the other, they softly cawed to one another.

"He has a gift," murmured Elan.

"He gives his gift willingly, it seems," responded Aleric.

"We shall see," came from Freya, skepticism faint in her soft voice.

"Voyeuristic fools," cackled Morigan. "Why do you bother to watch when you know the outcome?"

Hugin and Munin sat quietly, observing their fellow feathered friends, and the bodies twisting and turning below them.

As one, they turned when Coronis landed softly beside them on the branch, briefly ruffling her feathers.

"So, it has begun?" She cawed softly.

The muted calls between the murder drifted above the lovers tangled below them, oblivious to the conversation.

"Yes," responded Freya, "so it would seem."

"Don't be a hawk," Coronis chastised.

"I wasn't being a hawk," Freya replied, ruffling her feathers against the rain. "You stated the obvious; I was simply agreeing with you."

Coronis cocked her head left then right, her sharp eyes piercing the other female with a look of irritation.

A moan from the beings below caught their attention once more and all eyes turned toward the sound. They watched as the ungainly bodies writhed, pushing and rolling as one.

"How can they spend so much time on such a simple act?" asked Morigan. "And to what end?"

Coronis glanced around at the murder. Each crow seemed to be asking the same question with the tilt of a head or a clacking of their beaks.

"They do this for pleasure as much—if not more so—than for procreation," she explained. "They derive enjoyment from the mating ritual. Amusingly enough, they refer to it as animalistic desire."

The others cackled in response to this ridiculous explanation. Their own species was, in their collective opinions, much more practical. A brief flirtation followed by the cloacal kiss, and a swift, silent flight away. All of the sounds and movement below made little sense.

"Remember, this particular joining is important," Coronis said, reminding them of why they were gathered.

As one, they nodded.

Beneath the branches, Madeline was panting. Odin flipped her over on her stomach, her face pressed into the moss and leaves. Lifting her hips to meet his own, he held Madeline firmly as he pushed deep inside, pressing his weight and twisting his body against hers. He was lost in the pleasure of her wrapped around him; her heat and slick driving him closer to his own edge. He could smell the smoke between them, mixed with the steam rising from the forest floor. The canopy of branches above shielded them as the rain came down harder.

At the back of his brain, he knew that he'd lost sense of his purpose, the reason he was here with this woman. All he could see was the red of passion he felt as he moved inside her, reaching forward toward the peak of pleasure.

Above them, Hugin and Munin softly murmured to one another.

"He will only succeed if he remembers his duty," Hugin said.

"And he will only remember his duty if he remembers," replied Munin.

"Such a paradox," Elan interjected, clearly having been listening to their conversation.

The smell of smoke was rising through the branches and Coronis flapped her wings, getting the attention of the others.

"Soon," she crooned, "soon he will ignite the flames."

"And just how will he do this with all of this rain?" asked Elan.

"It is not our place to question how he can create the smoke and the flame," Coronis replied. "It is essential that we watch over and make sure he does."

"If he had just taken up with the woman by my name, we would not have to," began Freya.

"It is not our place!" Coronis snapped.

A loud, guttural sound from below stopped the crows' conversation. All eyes turned to look at the man and woman below them.

Odin, his face lifted to the sky, was crying out to his gods. His body stiffened as he reached his climax. The woman, Madeline, bent beneath him became a vessel for his seed.

Around them, the fire crackled and leapt from the ground up to the branches where the crows perched. Smoke enveloped them, momentarily hiding them from the birds' view.

Coronis took flight, quickly followed by the others; their caws announcing to all who could hear that the seed of Odin had been planted.

Cherry Street

Ian Withrow

"Hey, what about Cherry Street? Don't they still do jazz nights or whatever?"

Natalie wasn't even looking at her friends, instead double-checking her outfit in the mirror in her apartment. At five-foot she was much shorter than her companions. Her blonde hair, which normally hung to the middle of her back, was up in the messy bun where she'd put it sometime earlier in the day.

She took no shame in admiring herself, nodding in appreciation at the muscles she'd worked hard to grow. She examined herself with a confident gaze, over-all pleased with what she saw. A youth spent playing sports, coupled with a health-conscious attitude she'd been developing since high school, had lent her a fit, trim physique that she'd worked hard not to spoil as her academic workload had increased the past few years.

She turned this way and that, looking herself over. She wore a white crop-top, a pair of jean shorts, a pair of tasseled brown leather ankle boots, and, though the others didn't know it, a matching black and red lace underwear set.

Noa seized the moment, drowning out Presley's

groan with her enthusiastic clapping.

"Yes! Oh let's go, can we, *amada*?"

Her friend's Galician term of endearment always made her smile.

"You know what they say, the best way to get over the breakup is to be under someone else's bed!"

Natalie couldn't help but laugh at her friend butchering the idiom.

Noa, a fellow international student, may have arrived from Galicia at the same time that Natalie flew over from Germany, but she'd already fully assimilated.

She was chaos incarnate, the definition of free spirit and easily among the truest friends that Natalie had ever made. She was tall enough to be a runway model, and had no trouble keeping up with her pace. Her lean bronze body was wrapped in a flowing knee-length tye-dyed dress. Her thick dark hair, a bundle of sleek braids that extended past the small of her back, was bunched together with a similarly colored strip of cloth.

"Jazz is *old people* music," Presley whined.

"Presley, *you're* old," Noa chastised him casually.

Presley looked truly stung by the comment. Presley was the picture of American health: dirty blond hair and sunburned skin over a summer body, a bright shining smile, and a pair of startling blue eyes with an uncanny depth. His burnt orange button down, fitted, wine-red vest and black slacks gave him an air of youthful maturity.

"Excuse me? Thirty one is *not* old."

Noa realized she must have cut him deeper than she intended.

"No, *cariño*, sweetheart, you are not so old. Forgive me?"

She put on her best pout and Presley treated her with another eye-roll.

"Seriously, it's not gonna be half the party we'd find somewhere else..."

"Yes, which means zero chance of jerk-face college kids and a much quieter crowd."

Presley couldn't disagree, but he still complained most of the way to the bar.

Sure enough, the enticing notes of a lonely saxophone drew them to an ancient set of wooden doors. A brief ID check later and they stepped into the dimly lit confines of Cherry Street Bar and Grill. The tempo picked up as they crossed the threshold and headed for a corner booth. The addition of a muted trumpet and the trickle of a soft piano perfectly accented the dark wood and recessed lighting of the cozy establishment. The audience was a mixed bag of the mid-thirties crowd, graduate students, and the occasional clump of hipper-than-thou undergrads, no doubt only in attendance ironically.

Noa swayed gently, eyes closed to the rhythm of the music and a smile on her face. Natalie felt immensely more comfortable as well, few people here realized the strength and popularity of American Jazz back home in Germany.

"Fantastic idea, *amada*."

"Yeah, can't stop a party like this," mocked Presley as he flagged down a waitress.

The girls shushed him, at least until he ordered a bottle of merlot and some bruschetta for the table. One bottle turned to three, and the bar warmed from both the drink and the company. The entire group had a strong buzz, and their conversation rambled far and wide. The music picked up throughout the night and even this relatively quiet establishment started to fill up with customers. Fortunately, they were in no danger of being overcrowded anytime soon.

"I'm gonna do it, fuck it," Natalie said, interrupting Presley in the middle of an explanation of malicious compliance.

"Do...what?"

"I *told* you, I'm gonna sign up for that class trip."

Noa smiled at Presley's long sigh.

"What *Presley*, how's that different from what you're doing?"

He popped his mouth open but couldn't seem to find a retort.

"She has you there!"

Natalie pulled out her phone and navigated the school website until she found where to register. She looked at the electronic form, but hesitated.

"What's the harm anyway," she said, half to herself. "I've no idea if I'll ever have another chance!"

Presley's expression softened.

"Look Nat, all I'm saying is you've got such focus, such drive. You've done all you had to and you've walked the quickest, most efficient path up til now. I just don't want you to do something that might hurt your prospects is all I'm saying."

"Oh, Noa, did you know my *father* was joining us tonight?"

Noa howled with half-drunk laughter.

"Oh well fine," he fussed. "Do whatever you'd like. I'm just trying to help is all."

"Presley, I'm losing my mind. I haven't even started my thesis yet. What if I've gotten it all wrong?"

Noa gasped.

"*Amada*! You have not even *comezou*? What are you thinking?!"

"I want to! I just can't seem to...*begin* the damn thing."

Noa nodded, trying to understand but visibly confused.

"What is wrong, do you not want to do the anthropology anymore?"

"I dunno," Natalie mumbled, "I guess I just haven't figured out exactly what I want yet. Maybe that's why I'm still in school, you know? I just love the *feeling* of history, of society, of culture. Maybe I'm just having trouble narrowing down–"

She'd have continued but Noa was staring across the dance floor and shushing her.

"*Amada,* look! *Professor Sexy!*"

Sure enough Connor McCabe was just wandering in from the outside. He cut a fine figure in a black leather jacket and dark jeans and Natalie made no bones about admiring him. He paused a moment to remove his jacket and scan the room before working his way to the bar. They watched surreptitiously as he flagged down the bartender and, in short order, received a pair of martinis. Maybe it was the wine, maybe it was Natalie's nerves unwinding or her normally unshakeable confidence returning, but she flushed with heat at the sight of him.

"Well, looks like he's here with someone then. Or soon will be," Presley said matter-of-factly.

Noa narrowed her eyes at Presley.

"We don't know this for sure, *amada,* I think the spirits are favoring you. I do not care what *sourpuss* would say."

Presley pursed his lips.

"You know I hate that stupid nickname, and don't shoot the messenger."

"What does this mean, do not shoot messengers?" Natalie cut in, mostly to get them to shut up.

"It means it isn't his fault, he's just telling us what

he sees."

Noa frowned and gave a shrug for what might have been before turning back to her wine. Natalie's gaze lingered a moment longer before their conversation resumed, Professor McCabe all but forgotten.

Theoretically.

As the evening lengthened, however, Natalie couldn't help but notice that the second martini sat untouched even as the professor ordered and drank another two for himself. She caught herself appreciating the way his button down clung to his well-cared-for frame; the way his sleeves, rolled to his elbows, revealed muscular forearms and the hint of a tattoo sleeve on his right arm; Even the way he laughed and casually conversed with the bartender.

"That's it, *amada*," Noa said firmly as she drained her wine glass.

Natalie, who had been watching the professor, snapped back to the conversation at hand, afraid she must have missed something.

"Sorry, what's what?"

"You've been staring at the man for an hour, and you could do a lot worse when it comes to your *corrida*."

Natalie snorted into her wine glass, feeling silly for getting caught but far from ashamed.

"Well, you said it first, he's a *very* attractive man..."

"Yes, yes he is, *amada*."

Presley laughed.

"Sure, let's just start sleeping with faculty, right?"

Hearing it out loud, hearing the echo of her own thoughts, only served to stoke the fire inside of her.

"Well, if you insist."

Natalie stood, running her hands through her hair and giving it a soft, lightly tousled look. She turned and looked at Noa for approval, who winked and pulled out a tube of lipstick and a bottle of perfume from her purse.

"Irresitíbel love, here put this on."

The cherry-red lipstick made Natalie's eyes and dazzling smile pop, and a quick spritz of the perfume unleashed an exotic aroma of passion fruit and caramel.

"You *are* kidding, right?"

"Lighten up, Presley," Natalie chided. "Who cares, he's not even in my department."

Natalie moved to hand the items back to Noa, but she waved her back.

"Keep them, I'll get them back tomorrow."

The lioness that usually inhabited Natalie's petite body was fully roused. She was tame inside the cage of a relationship, but here in the wild she was returned to her natural element.

"Nat, come on. I'm all for a good time but this is just asking for trouble. You don't want to be the girl that sleeps with a teacher, do you?"

"As it happens, Presley, I don't need you to fight my

battles for me *or* lecture me on my life choices."

With that she stood and tugged the front hem of her shirt down a little. Her cleavage suitably revealed, she sauntered off in the direction of her prey.

Connor blinked with surprise as Natalie appeared beside him. She knew the effect she could have when she wanted, and was pleased to note his eyes dip to her chest before returning to her own.

"Well hello," Natalie purred.

"H-hello yourself. I'm, uh, actually-"

"Here with someone?"

Natalie finished his sentence while nodding at the second martini.

He gave an apologetic grin and nodded yes.

"Really," Natalie pondered aloud, allowing her hand to snake out and lift the cool drink from the bar top.

The glass left a ring of condensation behind on the dark wood, clear evidence it had been there a while.

"Your friend running late?"

"Uh, well–"

Natalie tipped the martini back and drained the glass, leaving a dark red stain on the rim and licking the last drops from her lips before setting the vessel back down.

"How about this, you can keep me company until your date shows up."

Connor's mouth was working, but he couldn't find

the words to counter the charismatic woman who seemed to have fallen into his lap.

"I dunno, I'm not really looking for–"

She put a finger to his lips, surprising him into silence.

"The question you should ask is what am *I* looking for?"

Connor was only human, and Natalie's charms were hard to resist.

"Alright, I'll bite. What are you looking for?"

Natalie relished his accent, and the smells of gin, stale cigarette smoke, and masculinity that clung to him.

"For now? Another martini."

He quirked an eyebrow, but Natalie could see his own desire building in the hunger in his eyes and the flush of his cheeks.

He hesitated, but only for a moment. Connor ordered two more martinis and turned his wry, charming smile back to his newfound date.

"Connor McCabe, a pleasure."

Natalie smirked.

"I'm sure you are, but names are for the morning after, no?"

Connor's eyes widened and he half-choked on his martini.

He shook his head softly and cleared his throat.

"Your accent, I'm not sure I can place it?"

"Germany, Niedersachsen, actually. Yours?"

"County Cork, Ireland."

"Hmm, I'd have thought to catch you drinking whiskey then, no? Isn't Ireland famous for it?"

Connor chuckled.

"Ah, you've found me out. Yes it is, but I never acquired the taste really. I suppose that's why they banished me."

Natalie's turn to laugh.

"Banished, eh? Is it a capital offense to forsake whiskey?"

"Oh, only in the presence of beautiful women."

Natalie's smile widened, she was delighted at his quip. Heat built in her chest and between her thighs.

"Oh is that so? Well, I promise not to tell your countrymen."

He nodded with faux solemnity.

"And you? What brings a beautiful Saxon maiden so far from her homeland, business or pleasure?"

"Pleasure, at the moment, Mr. McCabe."

"Professor, actually."

"Oh, *professor*, well excuse me. And what are you a professor *of*?"

"Nothing too terribly exciting, alas."

"Try me, you never know what might get me...excited."

She slipped a hand onto his thigh, kneading it

gently.

Connor looked her up and down again, allowing his eyes to linger before he pulled a pack of cigarettes from his pocket. He plucked a menthol from the pack and tucked it between his lips.

"I'm out for a drag, care to join me?"

Natalie reached slowly up, grabbed the cigarette from his mouth and leaned forward until she was whispering in his ear.

"You'd better pay your tab first, I'm not sure we'll be back."

Connor paid and allowed himself to be dragged from the bar by his hand. Natalie winked broadly at Noa as she passed and tried not to laugh at the sour look on Presley's face.

The air was warm, but not too humid. The stars were out and the rural air was relatively unspoiled. Natalie dropped Connor's hand and took a deep breath with her eyes closed. She opened them again and turned to the sound of the lighter in Connor's hand.

Natalie grinned and tucked her stolen cigarette into the corner of her mouth. She leaned forward and allowed Connor to light it for her. She took a pull as he lit his own and exhaled softly in his direction.

"So, have you been here long, Connor? May I call you Connor?"

He nodded and blew a slow, rolling smoke ring.

"You may, though I still don't know what to call you?"

She caught his sideways glance and pondered a moment.

"I'll keep you posted."

He nodded and took another drag.

"I never could get the hang of smoke rings."

Connor blew another large ring, then shot a smaller one through its center with a wink.

"The secret's in the tongue."

It was finally Natalie's turn to be tongue-tied and blushing.

She coughed to cover her surprise and hoped the darkness hid the flush in her cheeks.

"Oh, is that so!"

Connor nodded sagely.

He tried fruitlessly to teach her for several minutes before she was laughing too hard to continue.

"Ah well, we tried."

They settled into silence as they smoked. It wasn't uncomfortable, but there was a distinct air of tension to it. Natalie enjoyed the smolder of the smoke in her lungs and the pleasant tingle of menthol on her lips. She rarely smoked, but it was a vice she'd toyed with over the past decade or so. Tonight, given the circumstances, she decided it was worth it.

"So," Natalie said brightly, flicking the cherry of her

cigarette to the ground and tucking the used butt into a side pocket of her purse, "Did you drive tonight, or walk?"

Connor raised an eyebrow.

"Gorgeous, funny, and environmentally conscious? Can my night get any better?"

Natalie watched him do the same to his cigarette before answering.

"Oh I'm *sure* it can."

Connor gave a slight nod and headed off down the street with his hands in the pockets of his jacket.

"This way, I hope you're as brave as you act."

Nat wondered what he meant as she hurried after him. She wasted no time matching his pace and was about to ask him about his cryptic statement when he stopped in front of a coal black and cherry-red motorcycle.

"Here she is."

Of course he has a motorcycle.

Natalie could feel the flush in her breast and felt her pulse quicken.

"Problem?"

Natalie realized she hadn't said anything.

"Oh no, no problem at all," she said, her voice low and heavy with desire.

He smiled broadly and held out his jacket.

"Want this? It might get cold?"

She accepted and wrapped the overlage garment around herself. Natalie ran a finger across the shiny metal of the machine, enjoying the cool touch and the palpable energy from it.

"I haven't got any helmets," Connor announced as he mounted the bike and looked back at her.

Her small hands found easy purchase on his lean chest as she slid on behind him. The bike was bigger than anything she'd ridden before, and the power it displayed when he fired it up sent a thrill through her body.

"Don't worry, I'll hold on tight."

The roar of the engine and the rumble of steel between her legs had her weak with desire by the time they finally stopped in front of a low duplex across town.

She'd allowed her hands to slide lower as the ride had progressed, and they now sat at his waist. Her fingers were wrapped around the buckle of his belt and she was very aware of the growing tightness of his jeans.

He waited patiently for her to dismount before following suit. Connor led the way to the door, unlocked it, and waved her through the threshold. She took stock of the room she'd entered as he turned back to lock the door behind them.

The room was fairly spartan, its most prominent features being a pair of armchairs, a coffee table covered in books and scribbled-on papers, and a substantially sized flat screen against one wall. A pair of crowded bookcases and two other doors completed the furnishings.

"So, how bout a drink, Slim?"

Connor brushed past her, so close she felt the air between them tingle with electricity. She shivered and quirked an eyebrow at him.

"Slim?"

He chuckled as he moved through one of the doorways and into what looked to be the kitchen.

"It's ah, an old movie reference..."

"No no, I know. It was Lauren Bacall's nick-"

"-Name. Yeah," he finished his interrupted sentence the same time she did.

He poked his head back into the room with a pleasantly surprised look.

"How'd you know that?"

She just smiled in return.

He disappeared again, only to return a moment later with two small crystal glasses of amber liquid.

"Brandy?"

Natalie accepted the glass, swirling the half-inch or so of liquid around a few times before sipping it. The brandy was just above room temperature, sweet and aromatic.

Connor took a seat in one of the chairs, a wide, leather-bound affair that looked older than she was.

"So, you're a film buff?"

Natalie examined her seating options and chose the most provocative. She let her glass hang low, crossed the few feet to Connor and perched herself on his lap. She crossed her legs at the ankle and slipped an arm along the back of the chair behind his head to steady herself.

"Less a buff and more a casual fan of Mr. Bogart."

She carefully adjusted her bottom, knowing full well the gentle pressure and massaging effect she was having on her date. She could feel what promised to be a perfectly acceptable instrument beneath Connor's jeans.

His arousal fueled her own.

Her already high libido, compounded by the fact that she'd been unintentionally edging herself all day, had her soaked in moments.

"Speaking of fans," she mumbled softly, "you certainly seem to be a fan of *something*."

"Ah, well, you have me at a disadvantage. It's *much* easier for you to tell than it is for me."

Natalie smirked and polished off the last of her brandy with a deep swallow. She arched her back provocatively to place the glass on the coffee table without leaving his lap.

"So is that a—"

She interrupted him by leaning forward, her hands against his chest and her lips at his jawline. He stuttered to a stop as she gently kissed his neck, her deft fingers working to unbutton his shirt. She moved her kissing down his chest as it became visible, sliding to her knees at his feet while she did so.

She felt his hands reaching for her body but she

intercepted them, grasping each of his wrists lightly and pushing them to his sides. She tucked his hands under his thighs with a soft tisk-tisk.

She turned her attention to his belt, unbuckling it swiftly and unzipping the dark denim of his pants. She only pulled them down a foot or so, enough to get a better view of her target. His briefs kept his member pressed against his hip, but they quickly joined his jeans near his knees. She eyed her prize greedily. He was thicker than most she'd had and plenty long enough for her purposes.

His breathing was shallow, rapid, husky. She looked up at his face and could see it dripping with desire. It wasn't the only thing in the room doing so.

Natalie stood and took a slow, deliberate step backwards. She crossed her arms and gripped the hem of her shirt with both hands, pulling it up and over her head in one smooth motion as she turned to put her back to him, denying him the front of her lingerie. She heard him groan but she only smiled. She dropped her shirt to the floor and unbuttoned her shorts, enjoying his sharp intake of breath as she bent forward and slid them off her hips to the floor.

She turned back to face him, pleased at the sight of his pulsing erection. She could see his muscles tight and straining, but he kept his hands where she had put them.

The lace front of her panties did little to hide her neatly trimmed mound, with its dusting of light brown hair.

Nonetheless, she slid her feet apart, spreading her legs as she widened her stance. She ran her hands down her body, starting with her neck, down over her pert, lace-covered breasts, down her toned stomach past her hips and finally between her thighs. She let out a soft moan, partly of genuine pleasure and partly for the effect she knew it would have. Sure enough his cock jumped and his lips parted with lust.

She could practically hear his brain switching off as his eyes glazed over. She cat-walked towards him, her eyes locked on his. Natalie climbed atop him, her knees on either side conveniently pinning his hands to the seat. Her hands found the tops of his shoulders and she settled low on his lap, the front of her panties sliding against his shaft as she rocked slowly back and forth.

Connor mumbled something unintelligible so she leaned in close. Her breasts brushed against his chest as she brought her lips to his earlobe.

"What's that?"

His response was to hungrily move his mouth towards hers, but she blocked him with a hand on his chin. She shook her head gently and returned to nibbling at his neck.

She reached a hand down between them, gripping his shaft and massaging it gently up and down. He was trembling with excitement and her own body was demanding the satisfaction it had been denied all day. She raised herself up and slipped her panties to the side, guiding the head of his member to her entrance.

She enjoyed the feel of his head rubbing against her clitoris and briefly considered toying with him further, but she couldn't override her own desire. She exhaled softly, settling down onto him and instinctively rocking her hips as he entered her. Their shared excitement ensured he slid in easily, parting her lips and giving her the irreplaceable feeling of being filled completely.

She arched her back and rolled her neck, enjoying the feeling a moment before slowly raising and dropping herself in his lap. She could feel tension building in his body almost immediately, and she rode the high of knowing he was enjoying himself as much as she was.

She leaned slightly back, shifting the angle of her motion so that he pressed against her g-spot, rubbing across it with every thrust. Immediately her eyes rolled and she shivered with pleasure. Her breathing grew heavier from exertion, and she could hear his rise to match it.

She picked up her pace, the burn in her thighs no match for the exquisite, pounding waves of pleasure as she dropped down on him over and over again. With one hand on his shoulder for support, she moved her other first to her chest, then down between her legs. She slipped a finger on either side of her clit, rubbing up and down between her labia with every stroke.

She bit her lip to keep from crying out, closing her

eyes in concentration as she neared her climax. It sped towards her like a cliff, and before she knew it she was free-falling. She slowed and shuddered atop him, rubbing slow, tight circles around her pearl as she rode her orgasm to the end. About halfway through she could feel him start to pulse inside her, and felt hot warmth filling her. His neck muscles strained and he grunted softly as her trembling inside drove him over the edge as well.

She leaned forward, arms around his neck not only for support but to bring her near his ear again.

"Thank you, you have *no idea* how badly I needed that," she breathed into his ear.

He half-smiled, wordlessly panting his own satisfaction.

They stayed that way for a minute or so, content to bask in the glow of their exertions, but before long Natalie rose, tucking her panties back in place to avoid making a mess as she dismounted him.

"Do you mind if I take a shower here?"

She bent to grab her shirt and shorts from the ground where she had dropped them.

"No, no. Of course not! Just down the hall, first left."

She winked at him, certain he was watching her as she sauntered off to the bathroom.

It was small and utilitarian, but the towels were fluffy and when she turned on the faucet the water was piping hot in no time. She stripped out of her underwear and her bra and tossed them unceremoniously with the rest of her clothes on the tile floor of the small room. She took a look at the soap and shampoo selection while she was easing her muscles in the stream of hot water. Bar soap and generic shampoo would have to do, not that Natalie was particularly picky anyway.

Twenty minutes later she was pulling back the curtains and grabbing a towel from the rack beside the tub. The room was foggy with steam and she glanced at the mirror above the sink. With her finger, and a sly grin, she wrote a message across the clouded surface.

Thanks, look me up sometime if you'd like another. - N.S.

She cracked the door to the room and watched as cold air dissolved the rest of the steam, leaving her writing invisible until the next time he fogged the mirror. On a whim she took her phone out and pulled up the web browser. The sign-up form for the field trip was still open. She clicked through the prompts until she was greeted with a friendly message confirming her registration.

She finished toweling off with a broad smile and slipped back into her shorts, bra, and shirt. She skipped the underwear, knowing they'd defeat the point of her shower if she put them back on, and wandered back into the living room.

"That was fast," Connor greeted her.

He was standing now, shirtless but with his jeans zipped up and belted once more.

"I wondered, did you want–"

Natalie put a finger to her lips and shushed him.

"Don't, you'll ruin it."

He quirked an eyebrow.

"Ruin it? I'm just trying to–"

Natalie rolled her eyes and let slip a soft sigh.

"See? Ruined."

She looked around the room, making sure she hadn't forgotten anything, and headed for the door.

"See ya around, Connor."

"I still don't have your name, you know."

Kat and the Cream

Nadine Romack

Now, I wasn't one to usually sit in the dressing room and count bills. I'd always found it tacky, and Amber—the wonderful, *beautiful* dancer who had taught me everything I know—had made it clear that that was one of the easiest ways for people to take advantage of you.

Issue was, on a quiet night, there isn't always much to do. Monday nights had never really been known for their ragers at *Den of Desire*. Those that *did* come in didn't exactly have the big bills the weekend crowd did, but management wouldn't listen to the dancer's ideas of closing for just *one* day a week.

They were here to shake ass, not make demands.

So, there I sat, watching from the corner of my eye as Bella organized her fare by amount in neat piles and Dora clicked away on her phone, uncaring that all three of us were in the equivalent of negligees. Artemis was on stage currently, if the song I felt the bass for more than *heard* was any indication. Tapping on my phone absentmindedly, I checked the time: 10:25 pm.

In all honesty, I could leave and be just fine.

This last weekend's earnings were more than enough for my phone bill, car payment, and insurance. Z took care of everything else, and I was half convinced the other woman would murder me for even insinuating I could help pay for more.

Just as I bent to unzip my heels and slip back into street clothes to call it an early night, Joey shouldered open the door, letting in more of the music from the club before muffling it again as he shut it.

He didn't bother averting his gaze from the three of us, just skimming his eyes across the room until he locked eyes with me. Joey Orloff was one of the managers of *Den of Desire* and without a doubt my favorite. He always tried to take care of his dancers when management got a bit...much. I doubted there was anything that phased the man anymore. He could walk in on the entire staff having an orgy back here and I would bet money that he would simply blink and shut the door.

"Kat, you have a private dance," he said when I met his eye, "second floor, room six."

Rolling my eyes, I sat up. The second floor consisted of ten "suites" that offered clientele a bit more privacy to do...whatever, honestly. So long as you didn't burn the place down, make *Den of Desire* complicit in a crime, or hurt one of the staff members, management was happy to turn a blind eye if your money was good. I was pretty sure I'd once sucked a man off while he made an arms deal.

"I was about to call it a night," I complained, smoothing down my bodysuit's top as I stood. The maroon velvet ended just below my navel, giving about four inches to the lace "skirt" that showed off *everything* underneath.

"Their money's good," he shrugged.

"It fucking *better* be on a night this slow."

Joey, the gentleman he was, held the dressing room door open for me as I passed, swaying my hips as I walked. Another lesson Amber had taught me early on: every appearance is a show, even if you're not the one on stage. The black latex of the boots hugged my thick legs all the way from ankle to mid-thigh, the click of the heels lost in the music of the main room.

There was no point walking past the stage—the men who were in the audience seemed enraptured enough— and in all honesty? I liked having that air of being more powerful than them. I had promised myself I'd never be underfoot to a man again. *I* would be the one wearing the boots, ones they could only dream of kissing.

Climbing the narrow, metal-tread stairs was annoying in a pair of regular shoes, but I kept my head high, hands firmly on both railings as I made my way to the second floor. There was a larger lounge further down the runway that overlooked the stage and seats below, but just at the top of the stairs began the private rooms.

One...

Two...

Three...

Coming to a stop in front of the sixth room, I paused for just a moment, adjusting my skirt one last time and tossing my blonde extensions over my shoulders to give it a bit of the more blown out look I had styled it into before this shift.

Knocking once, I let myself in, tilting my chin up. The dark laminate floor mimicked walnut, and the plaster and brick walls were washed red by the LED lights. A high-backed white sectional took up one corner of the room, while a small fridge, a wall clock, a speaker, and pole took up another. I didn't need to look up to check the mirrored ceiling.

I knew it was a nice view.

The woman spread out on the couch in front of me wasn't half bad, either.

She had her hair shaved at the sides, with a bit of dark bangs splayed in front of her forehead. Her dark eyebrows cast her eyes into shadow, but even in the low red lights, it was obvious the hunger there.

Good.

I plastered on a smirk, making my way over and sitting at her side, putting one hand on the woman's chest, pushing her back a bit and enjoying the feeling of muscle underneath.

"Hi there, sweetheart. You can call me Kat," my voice was just above a purr as I leaned close to the woman, only a few inches from her face. "What can I call you?"

It was a trick question of sorts, I knew the woman in front of me as familiarly as I knew Ben Franklin's face.

Zoya Dmitrievna Vinogradova.

Boss of the Vinogradova syndicate.

Wanted in three countries.

Dealer in *all* things pleasure.

Also, the woman who signed my paychecks. Or well, the woman who signed the paycheck of the chump who signed my paycheck.

"You don't need to call me anything." Her accent was thick in a way that encircled me, squeezing my throat and heating me to my core.

I flicked my gaze up and down the client once before sitting back a bit, crossing my legs so that one heel grazed Vinogradova's leg.

"Alright then, and what is it, *exactly*, that you wanted? I'm all ears." Tattoos ghosted down the woman's neck, diving under the collar of her white shirt and peaking out from the open buttons across her chest and encircling her wrist. I wanted to see how far they went.

Vinogradova mirrored my quick glance before using the arm furthest from me to reach into the breast pocket of her tailored jacket and pull out a business card. No, not a business card, a *credit* card. Black. Metal.

She held it out casually between two fingers towards me.

Instead of taking it, I raised an eyebrow, trying to keep the confusion off my face. *I* was supposed to be in charge here, damnit.

"I thought you already paid." I *knew* she did. Joey wouldn't have told me to get up here if the payment hadn't gone through.

"I did. This is yours."

Now with *both* manicured brows raised, I extended one hand to take the card. It could be fake. She could cancel it tomorrow, and just wanted that power play of being rich and in charge. But *still*, it wasn't like I got to hold a *metal credit card* often in my life.

But just as my hand came up to snatch it, Vinogradova flicked it out of reach, closer to her chest.

This bitch. My smile dropped. At the change in my expression, the other woman smiled wide.

"It's *yours*, if you can win."

I narrowed my eyes, "Win *what?*"

"A wager."

"What kind?"

Vinogradova's smile sharpened.

"You're known for being...difficult," she said slowly. "You're in charge of everything the audience sees. No one does *anything* without your approval. You may be a whore on your knees, but you can still bite. I like that." She looked at the card between her fingers. "No limit on this card. No expiration. No strings attached. It's yours if you win."

"The wager?"

"Patience, Kat," Vinogradova hummed. "Yes, the wager." At that, she leans closer, so now she's the one invading my space, instead of the other way around. "I bet *this* card, that I can have you unraveled and begging in 10 minut–"

"I don't *beg*."

Another hum. "If you win, it's yours."

"And if you win?"

"When I win, I'll have the satisfaction of knowing I had the beautiful Katherine Harrison writhing underneath me."

When, not if. She was cocky. I wasn't sure if that pissed me off or made me wet.

"Do we have a deal?"

Dealer in all *things pleasure.*

I narrowed my eyes, before relaxing fully, my smile coy—rehearsed. "I'm already thinking about what I'm buying first when that card's in my purse."

Suddenly there were two hands on my hips, pulling me off of the couch and leaving me braced above the other woman.

Flicking against the string off my thong, both of her thumbs rubbed soothing circles on my bare hips. The rough pad of her finger so different from the smooth, sensitive skin there.

"Can I kiss you?" Vinogradova asked.

My breath stuttered as I grasped for my stage persona to save face. "That costs extra."

"Put it on my card."

Surging up, Vinogradova's lips were on mine, licking into my mouth and nipping at my bottom lip with enough force to toe that line between pleasure and pain. Taking advantage of my surprise she deepened the kiss, her touch trailing down my hips to my thighs and leaving goosebumps in her wake.

When we pulled apart, the other woman attached herself to my jawbone, kissing and sucking on my neck as she made her way down.

It's not acting, the way I moan for her mouth on me. My every nerve was on fire under her hands and mouth.

The tip of her tongue, the whisper of a kiss, trails down from behind my ear to my pulse point, then that bit of skin where my shoulders meet my neck. She bites down hard at the juncture, sucking with a force I know will leave a mark for everyone to see when I leave. A mark I'll have to cover with makeup all week. Somehow, I can't bring myself to mind.

"You make such pretty noises," she whispers against my skin. "I'm going to hear all of them tonight," she promises.

One of my hands rises from its place on her shoulder, acrylic nails lightly dragging up the back of her neck and sinking into her dark brown hair. Wrapping my fingers around it I rip her head back as her hands return to rest on my hips.

"You're talking a big game from just a few kisses," I glared down at her.

"Zoya."

I raised an eyebrow at her, the woman in question just sitting there, resting her head against the hand still grasping her hair.

"You asked earlier what you can call me."

"You said it was unimportant."

"Yes, but I've decided when you scream out, I want it to be my name on your lips."

With her eyes still on mine, her hands grasped my hips and pulled me down until my crotch made contact with her thigh. She flexed once, the pressure brushing against my clit. I bit back a gasp.

Slowly, she dragged me back, keeping my pelvis flush with one of her spread legs. Taking a shaky breath, I relax my face, my hands sliding down to lace behind her neck. I had a metal credit card—not to mention my own ego—on the line. I needed to keep my cool.

Raising an eyebrow at my silent challenge, Zoya dragged me forward again, flexing her thigh as she moved me. The texture of the lace of my thong added to the friction of her black pants against my core. It was *delicious*.

"Do you get wet for every pervert who pays you, or am I an exception?"

"You wish this was all for you," I bit out. One of her hands immediately left my hip just to smack my ass.

"I'm starting to realize I am not that big a fan of brats."

"Then you should have paid for someone else's time," I ground out, my clit grinding against the center seam of her slacks.

A huff.

"And miss out on all of this? Never." With the same hand she spanked me with, she took my chin between her thumb and forefinger, not speaking again until our eyes locked. "I can feel how hot you're getting through my pant leg. Are you going to make a mess of yourself?"

I didn't answer at first, because I honestly didn't know how to answer. It wasn't the first time I had been back in these VIP rooms, putting on a show or making someone else cum in their pants. I just never cared for losing myself in front of a stranger. The awkward walk back down the stairs just to go wipe myself up with wet wipes in the dressing room was a deterrent as well.

But the way this woman looked at me, a mixture of hunger and worship, felt like it was consuming me whole. The purr of her voice slid down my spine like silk. And the string grip of her fingers digging into my thigh? The weight of her palm on my ass?

Grinding myself down on her thigh, I nodded.

Her smile grew dangerous, her hands on my hips like iron chains, bringing me to a halt.

"No."

I stared at Zoya incredulously.

"Fucking excuse me?" It was an *honor* to see me cum in a VIP room. The fuck did she mean *no*?

She clicked her tongue, shaking her head and furrowing her brow in mock admonishment. "Language, Kitty Kat." Her smile was mocking. "Ask me nicely, and I'll consider it." Her eyes flicked over my shoulder. The clock.

Beg, she said without outright saying it.

I reached for the stage persona and grasped it with both hands. I could be in charge, I *would* be in charge. I gritted my teeth. Two could play this game. I was walking out of here with deeper pockets *and* an orgasm.

Dropping my head down to brush my lips against the shell of her ear, I ground my hips down again.

"I think you'll like seeing me cum, Zoya," I whispered. "I'll moan so pretty for you. I'll shake and gasp right here in your lap. Not many people get to see me like that, you know."

Zoya takes a deep breath underneath me and I bite back my smile.

"They won't mind if we stay longer, you know," I murmur against her skin, grinding down again and squeezing my legs around her thigh. "And once I come for you, I'll make you come for me. Maybe on my tongue? What about my fingers? I'll do either for you. I'm sure you'd make pretty noises, right, *Zoya*?" I held out her name, flicking it up at the end just as I ground myself down as firmly as I could. All I can picture as I'm saying this is me on my back. Her fingers, her tongue in me, crooking *just* so until I see stars and am oversensitive.

I'm there, I am *right* there.

She's ruined me, and she knows it.

The hands on my hips squeeze me once before stopping my movement.

It was her turn to tangle a hand in my long blonde hair, gripping at my skull and pulling me back until my back arched to an obscene degree. She bit the side of my tit that was exposed in the low-cut top as if in reprimand before leaving open mouthed kisses down my sternum. Tilting my head, my eyes caught on the large clock that was supposed to be simultaneously a reminder of time in the VIP rooms as well as "decoration."

10:42.

I blinked. It had been more than ten minutes. A quick smirk overtook my lips before I could control my face, rolling my torso in a way that pulled Zoya closer. Who's to say I couldn't have my cake and eat it too?

I ground myself down again on her thigh, harder than before. It wasn't the most comfortable position but fuck it, I had been on the edge since this wager began and every ounce of friction pushed me closer.

A click of a tongue. The hand in my hair tightened, pulling me forward until my forehead was pressed against her's. We locked eyes.

"Did I say you could cum?"

"I think you should."

I felt her eyebrow raise more than saw it with how close we were.

"And why is that?"

"Because I cum here, and I'll let you take me home for round two. And three. And maybe four if your strap is as good as your mouth."

Zoya was silent for a moment, considering.

"Did I say that nicely enough?" I asked innocently. I felt her free hand tighten on my thigh in reply.

"If I remember correctly, *Brat*, I told you to ask me nicely. That didn't sound like you were asking. I don't take demands from whores."

I pulled my face back for just a moment to blink doe eyes at the woman before I leaned so far forward that we were sharing the same air.

"Please?" I whispered against her soft lips.

I felt the moment under me where whatever control Zoya still had snapped. Her tongue toyed with mine as one hand snaked down, digging her palm against my cunt. It would be so easy for her to pull my thong to the side and push one finger in. But Zoya Vinogradova had never been an easy woman.

When my orgasm hit, it was more of a crash. My body had been pulled taught from the tension and albeit collapsed against the strong arms underneath me. Zoya didn't do anything but hold me through the aftershocks. Minutes passed like that.

The silence of the room was punctuated by the bass of the music down below and my ragged breathing.

"How are you feeling?" Zoya asked, her voice muffled by my hair.

"Like you just ruined one of my good thongs."

A snort. "You don't wear your good underwear on weeknights." A pause, then, "Is your bag packed downstairs? I can make Orloff bring it up here for you."

I mumbled what I thought sounded like a yes, but was too busy lying boneless on the other woman's lap. I felt simultaneously drained and like I was still sitting on a live wire. My thong—or at least what wasn't sucked into my ass crack—was soaked through.

A clipped knock. The door opened. The thump of a duffel bag being dropped just inside the room. The door shut. Another kiss to my temple.

"*принцесса*, let's get you changed. We have leftovers at home I can heat up for you."

That finally got me to sit back a bit, my glare not as heated as I would prefer as my facilities came back online.

"Leftovers? *Leftovers?* You just made me ride your thigh and cum from *nothing* other than my clit. Fuck off. Use my card and buy me dinner."

Zoya raised an eyebrow at me. "*Your* card?"

With a small smile, and whatever was left of the bratty persona I had, I patted the woman's chest before getting to my feet and walking over to my bag.

"Yes, *my* card. I'm hungry. We're ordering pad thai."

A snort.

"Yes, dear."

Beasts of Beauty and Burden

Jemma G. Vale

"Damnit Lou, he tore up the couch, *again!*" The blonde woman groaned, standing in the doorway, black booted foot tapping an irritated beat on the hardwood floor.

Across the room, another woman with auburn hair and an impish—if not apologetic—smile, crouched down next to a dark fur covered form. "Oh Petra, love, he didn't mean it...you know how storms make him anxious!" Her blue eyes were wide and pleading.

From afar the form may have resembled an enormous dog, but if one were to get close enough they would see a creature that was some sort of hybrid monstrosity. Ever since Dorian had wandered into their lives, Petra had always thought he was terribly ugly, at least in this form. Body shaped much like a bear's; fur that was dark with spotted patches on his haunches, legs and the thick mane around his neck; large feline claws that could rip and tear, with teeth to match; horns growing out of his massive head; and a face sort of like a bison. To Petra, he looked like something that had crawled out of her nightmares, but to her wife, Lou...

"Look at this face, Petra! How could you be mad at such a sweet face?" Lou crooned as she upturned the male's face towards her wife. And to Dorian's credit his hazel eyes darted down to the floor like a puppy trying to show how ashamed he was for pissing on the floor.

Petra's mouth turned to a hard line as she gave her wife a skeptical look."You and I have very different definitions of a *sweet face...*" She hissed, crossing her arms.

Lou clicked her tongue in disapproval before turning back to the furry form next to her and placing a kiss on his forehead. Dorian made a low grunting sound and buried his face against her side, breathing turning into nervous snuffling against the fabric of her skirts.

Petra stifled another groan.

She ran a hand over her face in exasperation, amber eyes narrowed. *She's lucky she's cute,* she thought to herself.

Petra sighed, tone softening into something playful, if not a little defeated."Well you're the witch here, just make sure to fix it, ok, princess?" She said, stepping closer to plant a kiss on Lou's smiling mouth.

Lou stood on tiptoe, pressing her lips firmly to Petra's and let out a soft happy hum at the kiss. Petra was damn near a foot taller than her and it made her feel so tiny despite being the curvier of the two. She hadn't realized that she had pressed her entire body against her wife until she felt both of their chests heave and their breathing hitched, becoming ragged. Her pulse hammered in her ears so loudly she had almost forgotten the rest of the world, until a large boom of thunder sent Dorian into a panic and brought her back to earth.

She almost whined when Petra pulled back, leaving her panting and eager, wanting much more as there was still a heat at her core just waiting to be turned to pleasure.

"I'm going to go lay down, work was rough." Petra sighed as she slipped past, shrugging off her raindrop speckled leather jacket and made her way into the bedroom.

Lou watched her go, and felt her shoulders sag."Dammit..." She mumbled.

With a whine, Dorian butted his head against her hand and she blinked, realizing she had momentarily forgotten that he was there. She gave him a smile before kneeling down to his level.

"She doesn't dislike you, I promise. She's just a little rough around the edges, and takes time to trust. Plus this *is* the third time you've chewed up the furniture..."

Dorian grunted, dark hazel eyes glimmering with a despair that nearly brought her to tears.

"My poor sweet boy," she said again, hugging him as the storm outside raged on.

***

The next morning the couch was indeed fixed.

Petra was pleased to see as much, but less than pleased to see the naked, albeit covered, man sleeping there. His brown hair was fluffed up like the seeds of a dandelion. His tan skin spotted with freckles.

Petra huffed. At least in this form he was nicer to look at.

Lou sang out from the kitchen."Good morning, darling!" Her voice was accompanied by the familiar sizzle of cooking food.

Petra chuckled and continued on, past the sleeping lump and into the kitchen. Lou stood at the stove, cast iron pans filled with a mish mash of eggs, vegetables, and seasoned meats. Fresh fruit sat in bowls on the kitchen island, colorful and inviting.

Petra popped a blueberry in her mouth then leaned down over her wife's shoulder, and planted a kiss on her rosy cheek.

"Good morning, my love," she whispered tenderly.

Lou shimmied her shoulders, a happy shiver ran through her. She was adorable when she was flustered and Petra loved to get her going. She began to trail kisses from her wife's cheek down to her jaw, then up, until she could nibble on her ear, a throaty laugh escaping as she did so.

Lou turned off the stove and pressed into her wife. She'd been left wanting the night before and all this teasing was only reigniting the embers of that same fire. Petra could see it in her face as she bit her bottom lip and looked up with her big beautiful eyes, long lashes batting delicately.

"P-pet–" Lou stuttered out.

Petra felt her own heart stall and then thunder in her chest, seizing her wife's chin in her hand and grinning like a fox. "Yes, my darling?" She breathed the words, low and husky.

Lou's cheeks puffed and further reddened. "Don't act as if you don't know," she pouted.

Petra tsked, ever so slightly tightening her grip on her love's chin, "I don't think I do, perhaps if you ask nicely though…"

Lou huffed and Petra could practically see the fog rolling in her wife's brain as lust filled her eyes, and made her body tremble.

"Petra, please…."

"Please, *what*?" she teased.

She wasn't about to make things easy on Lou. She was the one that wanted Dorian to stay. And it was his…affliction that had thrown a wrench in their sex life, so she felt it was only fair for her to bait her a bit, hold out just a little longer, even if it was killing her too. Her own stomach flipping in anticipation of what was coming.

Lou whimpered, "Please make me feel good."

That was enough for Petra.

Rougher then she meant to, she moved her wife so she was facing her and pressed between her body and the counter. She kissed her deeply and shivered when she felt Lou's pleading moans against her mouth. Gods, she had needed this. She pushed her knee up, pressing between Lou's legs and putting a pleasant amount of pressure there, earning more soft cries of pleasure as she felt her wife's hips jerk and grind, the movements frantic and eager. She felt Lou's hands fist in the back of her grey sweater, keeping her close, her tongue tracing across Petra's.

She needed more. She turned Lou back around pinning her hips with her own, and kissed her neck. Lou whined and pressed her ass back. Petra sputtered out a husky laugh at the glare she was getting as she rolled her sleeves up, her wife's impatience was absolutely intoxicating to her.

Petra carefully wrapped her arms around Lou. "Greedy, greedy," she said, before drawing up the front of her night gown and being pleased that there were no other barriers between her fingers and the inviting wetness of her wife's pussy.

She traced her long pale fingers along the folds before slowly, almost painfully, moving, pressing forward until she was rubbing at her clit. Teasing at first as she relished the gasp she received, and then she couldn't hold back anymore. She bent Lou over the kitchen island as she plunged her fingers in and out of her, she wanted to be touched too but just experiencing Lou's pleasure right now was enough. Fuck, she loved this woman, loved the way her body felt against her, the wailing cries of pleasure she made, the flushed looks as she cried out her name, and especially the way she tasted.

Thinking of her taste, she retracted her fingers, Lou nearly sobbing in frustration, and she brought them to her lips, licking them clean.

"P-petra!" her wife's voice came out wobbly.

Petra lowered herself to her knees."Shhhh, I'm nowhere near done with you, my love," she promised. "Stay still now." She purred as she moved her mouth to Lou's sopping wet entrance and used her tongue to replace her fingers.

"*Fuck!*" Lou yelped and pressed her hips back.

Petra hummed, a contented note as she thought about what a happy little puddle her lover would be when she was done, an absolute babbling mess–

Lou sucked in another breath but this time it wasn't one of pleasure but surprise, and another sound. A low whimper and heavy breathing.

Petra's head whipped up to see a groggy Dorian, throw blanket wrapped haphazardly around his hips, but doing nothing to hide the erection he had. His tanned face was crimson as he stared openly at the two.

Petra bared her teeth, her own cheeks heating as her back straightened.

"Dorian..." Lou whispered, her voice still trembling but now sounding shy.

Petra felt a pang of jealousy as she realized her wife's eyes were fixed on Dorian's erection tenting the purple knit blanket he was barely covered with.

It wasn't that she was against another partner or a third joining but...

Petra sneered, "Ever heard of knocking?"

Dorian flinched and his gaze focused on Petra. She had expected his eyes to grow cold or wary, maybe even hateful when they had turned from her wife and to her but...strangely enough the burning hunger he had looked at Lou with remained as he looked her over as well, if not a bit more hesitantly. She watched him bite his lip and then look away, his hand gripping the blanket around his waist a bit tighter.

Dorian couldn't speak. This had been true since he had shown up at the woman's remote forest cottage. Whether in his day time human form or his cursed night time form, He was unable to utter a word. He could write though, but she felt like the man would be too embarrassed to write out his thoughts at this moment.

Lou shivered. "Petra?" She said, looking down at her wife who still kneeled on the tiled floor behind her.

Petra let her eyes slide up to her wife's wide eyes, and knew what she wanted. She'd known it was coming for a while. It wasn't uncommon for them to take extra partners to bed, men, women, human, witch, the occasional forest dwelling creature. She had never minded and had fully expected this to happen at some point but...Dorian was different. He wasn't some random passerby, someone looking for a transactional fuck, or a friend. Lou had come to care for the man over the months they had taken him in. Originally it had been to try to break his curse. A nasty thing born of rejection and hate, put on him by an obsessed woman from his past that he hadn't known was a witch.

Every day. Every day Petra had seen that affectionate look in her wife's eyes grow into something more.

And as much as she acted like she hated having him around, he *had* grown on her too. Maybe not as much as her wife but she couldn't deny she felt the need to protect him and care for him as well. Maybe it was why she had been out on so many late night jobs lately. She was a bounty hunter, and she was using all of those skills to secretly hunt down the bitch that had cursed their idiot.

Their idiot.

Fuck.

Petra took a deep breath. She ignored how hot her cheeks felt, and the anxious pit in her stomach. She looked back at Dorian, forcing his gaze to meet hers, "Living room. No blanket, sit in the big arm chair."

He stared at her for a moment, as if he were trying to decipher the words of someone speaking another language, before it clicked and he stiffened. He looked to

Lou who only nodded emphatically, her body once again shaking in anticipation. Dorian turned on his bare heel before another word could be spoken, probably scared Petra would change her mind and the sound of the blanket falling to the ground could be heard as he retreated.

Petra chuckled and rubbed at her eyes.

"Are you sure?" She heard Lou whisper, worried.

She stood smoothly and gave her wife a playful smile."Yes, my love, you know me. I wouldn't have said it if I wasn't," she mused, as she reached out and smacked her bare ass. "Now follow me to the living room before I change my mind?"

Lou watched her, looking for any trace of hesitancy before nodding. "You're amazing, you know that?" She said, an adoring half smile forming on her beautiful mouth.

Petra snorted as she pulled her sweater off and started towards the other room, "Hey now I'm doing this as much for myself as you, you've had me on the edge all week, you tease."

Lou's giggle rang out like a bell as she followed, the tension in her turning purely sexual.

Dorian had obeyed Petra's previous command. He sat on the large arm chair, and was still erect, looking like he didn't know how to sit still. Petra swore she could see him vibrating. When his eyes fell on them again she was in nothing but a black thong and bra. That look of desire only intensified. Petra knew she was attractive but she still found herself surprised at just how much he seemed to want her. She felt Lou's arms wrap around her from behind, mirroring how she had hugged her lover in the kitchen.

Petra looked down at Dorian, and *fuck* he was big. She had seen him naked plenty of times by now, but never erect and usually she tried not to look at his cock. Admittedly, she had snuck glances at his ass a few times and could confirm it was a nice one. She reached out slowly and kept eye contact as she traced the fingers that had been inside her wife only moments before around the head of his dick. She watched him shiver and bite his lip. It was a cute expression and she could feel Lou watching, mesmerized, behind her.

"I'm going to ride you while I eat out my wife. Got it?" She said, voice gentle but commanding.

Dorian's eyes widened but he nodded, spreading his legs a bit to give her a better angle.

Petra was already so wet. She had woken up aroused that morning, and her time in the kitchen with her wife had left her soaked. She carefully turned, pulling her thong down and letting it fall to the floor before she eased her hips down, lining Dorian's erection up with her opening and slowly, sinking down. Dorian's hands flew to her hips, gripping them carefully. He did not attempt to move her or keep her in place, but she felt his thumbs absently rub circles into her skin, and it felt really good.

"Good boy," she rasped as she sank down on him completely, feeling him slide home.

Lou made a strangled sound of pure lust, watching them as she touched herself.

"Ah, ah. None of that," Petra said, reaching out and pulling her wife forward by her wrists. "Put your foot here so I can get a good angle, princess." She whispered, patting the arm of the chair.

Lou whimpered but did as she was told.

When Petra had them all adjusted to where she wanted them she clenched her pussy tight around Dorian's dick giving him a jolt of pleasure, "I hope you're both ready because I'm not going to take mercy on either of you."

The two looked at each other before she was a blur of movement. She began to move her hips, grinding them into Dorian's, and clenching her muscles rhythmically as he pounded in and out of her and she simultaneously buried her face in her wife's wet slit. Both made the most wonderful noises, and her wish to be touched was most certainly granted as she felt hand on her. One of Lou's was in her hair, pulling and tugging and the other seemed to be resting carefully in the middle of her shoulder blades, keeping herself steady. Dorian's were on her hip still until she felt one of his arms snake around her slender frame and down between her legs until she felt his fingers find their way to her clit. She went rigid for just a moment before she moaned against Lou's thigh momentarily.

Lou chuckled before Petra's tongue had her crying out once more. Petra would have them cumming before they could have a coherent thought.

Petra gasped as Lou pulled her hips back and away from her eager mouth. A look of lust and mischief danced in her eyes as she smiled down at her,

Petra licked her wet mouth, "What are you doing, my love?"

"I think it's time you got to be pampered, darling." she said, caressing Petra's face gently before sinking to her knees.

"Lou–" she started before feeling Dorian's strong arms wrapped around her and pulled her back, using his legs to spread hers more, leaving everything out to bare to her kneeling wife.

She gasped and shook, her pussy clenching as she became more aroused, "D-did you two plan this or something?"

"No, but we both know you need some extra attention," her wife purred, kissing both her and Dorian's thighs.

Petra blew out a breath she hadn't realized she was holding as she watched her wife's lips draw closer until they were at that sensitive bundle of nerves. She watched and felt her kisses before her tongue dragged lazy circles there and had her bucking on Dorian's cock. He got a better grip and moved her hips slow and rough, she realized he was now rubbing pleasantly and persistently on her G spot and she cursed. Lou giggled, and her hand made its way up Petra's stomach to cup her breast and play with her hardened nipples.

"She likes her tits played with, Dorian dear, and if you bite her neck at the same time..."

"L-lou!" She gasped, just as Dorian's hand moved to the opposite breast and began to tease, and his lips and teeth grazed the sensitive skin of her neck. She wasn't used to being ganged up on like this.

Oh they are so in trouble...

But this time she could tell she had to admit defeat. The myriad of sensation and pleasure was too much.

"*Fuck*, I'm going to cum," she cried, her hips losing their rhythm as the fog that accompanied a growing orgasm began to take over.

She cried out as the mix of mouths and hands, and the cock she bounced on, brought her to completion. And a scream of pure pleasure was ripped from her lungs. Wetness pooled between her thighs.

She felt like all the strength in her body had been drained and she let Dorian cradle her against his chest.

Lou beamed with pride as she licked away the evidence of her wife's pleasure. "Wow, I don't think I've seen you cum that hard since we had that water nymph over!" She remarked proudly.

Petra snorted, reaching back to pet Dorian's hair, "You didn't finish did you?"

She hadn't felt the familiar feeling of cum filling her up.

Dorian buried his face against the crook of her neck and shrugged, obviously embarrassed as she could feel him throb inside her.

Petra hummed, continuing to pet his hair, "Don't worry, we're not done."

He looked like he wanted to protest but Petra turned and planted a kiss on his mouth. It didn't matter that he couldn't speak, it just felt right as it was what she did anytime she wanted Lou to stop arguing.

Petra eventually broke the kiss and stood on baby deer legs and relished the feeling of Dorian sliding out of her.

"Lay on the floor," she told him.

He blinked, dazed still from the kiss, earning another round of giggles from Lou, and a mumbled "so cute."

When he was down she winked at her wife and moved to kneel over the man's face and Lou sank down onto his twitching erection.

They spent the next hour riding his face and cock until he finally came. When he did they all laid sprawled on the floor, slick with sweat and cum, and all breathing heavy but content.

"I suppose I could get used to this..." Petra mumbled as she closed her sleepy eyes.

"Yeah?" Lou asked, excitement thick in her voice.

"Hey as long as I don't have to replace the couch and you do your magic thing...Yeah."

The idea of committing Dorian to the innermost workings of their relationship definitely made Petra nervous. So for now, she would deny that it was totally permanent.

Inside though, she felt like maybe, just maybe, there was enough room in their home, bed, and even hearts for Dorian.

Our Idiot.

A Study of Passion

Siobhan Johnson

"Shh," he whispered, and laid a finger against her lips. Leaning forward he brushed his lips alongside her cheek, whispering as he did so, "Sammy."

Gently, he put his fingertips on her chin and titled her face up to his. Their lips met briefly, just the lightest of caresses. He looked at her and saw she had closed her eyes. She swayed toward him and he slipped his arm off the back of the couch and around her shoulders, pulling her close. He felt her body respond, her nipples harden.

Samantha's head was swimming. *She couldn't blame it on the wine, could she?* She asked herself; she had only had a couple of glasses before he'd gotten there. Yet, she wanted this man.

When he reached up and caressed her neck, running his fingers along her jaw line and down her throat, she arched her back a little as if to ask him without words to unbutton her dress. She wanted him to pull the soft green material aside to kiss her breasts, caress them through the thin fabric of her bra before unfastening and pushing it aside. Her body was giving her away; her nipples, taut and at attention.

Jake watched as Samantha, eyes still closed, arched

her back and sighed at his touch. He wanted to unbutton her dress and release her breasts from the confines of its fabric. He felt her arousal in the flush of her skin. Leaning forward again, he kissed her full on the mouth and gave a small moan when she opened to him, tasting him as he tasted her.

Samantha's senses were heightened. Every nerve in her body was alive. She hadn't felt this madness for ages. Charles had needed her occasionally, to release his want but he had almost stopped making love with her over a year ago. Their sex had become just that, sex; no magic, no passion, just get it done sex—the Thursday before his death was the closest they had come to making love in a long time. This was different, perhaps because it was new, the two of them new to each other. They both opened their eyes and found the other watching.

Without words, Samantha began to unbutton her dress to reveal a forest green front close bra and matching forest green panties. Jake stopped her hands at the bra and unfastened it himself, pushing aside the fabric and tracing her nipples with his thumbs.

"You're beautiful," he whispered, looking her in the eyes.

She whimpered as he lowered his head and kissed first one and then the other of her nipples. He shifted her, leaning her against the arm of the couch, one hand caressing its way down her belly to the edge of the thin satin fabric covering her curls, the other cradling her head. He showered her neck and shoulders with kisses, moving back to her mouth and nibbling on her lips.

Samantha's breathing became shallow as Jake's hand touched her intimately, caressing and stroking her through the fabric before pulling it down enough to slide his fingers beneath to touch her flesh. She gasped at the sensations flying through her. Jake moved his hand and Samantha's body arched against him and shuddered. Continuing to move his fingers in small circles around her arousal, Jake kissed her again, their tongues doing an intimate tango.

Coming slightly to her senses, Samantha reached up and began to unbutton Jake's shirt, trying to be careful not to pop them in her haste to touch his bare flesh. Pulling his shirt from his waist band, she kissed him as she tugged at the zipper of his khakis, sending a silent prayer of thanks for his lack of a belt. She could feel his hardness through the material and wanted to wrap her fingers around him. Raising his hips slightly, Jake helped her rid him of his slacks and boxers, his shoes already cast aside.

"Sammy, baby," Jake whispered again, his voice catching in his throat when she touched his bare flesh. "Are you...?" he began before she hushed him with her mouth.

"Don't talk," she whispered into his mouth, "not yet; not now. Please, I want you, yes," she breathed against his neck as he pushed between her legs.

From the moment he pushed inside her, Jake's body took over, his mind lost in the heat of her body. They moved together, finding a frenzied rhythm, their desire to get closer, to push deeper overwhelming them both.

Samantha's cry of pleasure brought him to the edge, hurtling him over before he could stop his release.

Spent for the moment, Jake rested his forehead against hers.

"I'm sorry about that," he muttered, embarrassed about his quick climax.

"Don't be," she whispered. "I don't think either of us could have held back. I certainly couldn't...didn't."

Her voice held just the slightest hint of amusement and he blushed.

Awkwardly, they situated their bodies next to one another on the couch.

"Why is it we can find our way in blind passion but once that rush is over, we fumble with the easiest things?" she asked, not holding back her laughter as she attempted to sit up.

"I have no idea," he laughed in return, his embarrassment replaced by amusement as he, too, tried to get comfortable.

Samantha laid her head against his shoulder as he finished adjusting himself. Eyes closed, she trailed her fingers down his chest, not daring to go any lower.

"Give me a few minutes and we can try again," he said softly, "I promise to take my time..."

"Hey, you weren't the only one in a rush," she said, interrupting him with a finger on his lips. "I don't know what it is about you...well, yes, I do," she corrected herself. "You are a very attractive man."

"Just after me for my looks, huh?" He teased.

"Who said I am after you?" She shot back.

"I just meant..." he stumbled over the words.

"I'm teasing you, Jake."

"As I was saying, you are a very attractive man—and it isn't just your looks. You are caring and intelligent. You're easy to talk to, and, as it turns out, you're a pretty good lover," Samantha continued.

Jake gave a soft growl as he leaned in and kissed her.

"Oh you haven't experienced anything yet," he told her, his eyes darkening as he pulled her close for another kiss.

"Oh really?"

It was the last thing she was able to say before he covered her mouth with his.

They made love by the firelight and when they were both exhausted, they lay in silence, lost in each other's arms.

Hours later, Samantha woke on the couch in the study, naked and covered with the quilt her

great-grandmother had given to her grandmother who had
given it to Samantha's mother and which Samantha had
received as a wedding present. Disoriented at first, it took
her a few minutes to remember what had transpired. Her
body flushed with the memory, shifting from embarrassed
mortification to plain embarrassment to mildly amused to
highly amused and ending with a strong urge to do it all
over again. Who would have thought an accountant could
be so passionate? *There you go with stereotypes*, she
chastised herself. Jake Stephen Palmer is anything BUT
your stereotypical accountant!

Her memory ran through the scenes from the night
before, smiling as her body reacted with a heat that began
in her midsection and spread up and down. Closing her
eyes, her fingers re-traced the path Jake's fingers had taken
when he had first touched her. She sighed out loud before
it registered that she may not be alone. Sitting up and
wrapping the quilt around her shoulder, she realized she
could smell coffee.

Looking around for her clothes, she saw nothing of
the dress she'd been wearing last night, nor her bra or
panties. A little alarmed at this discovery, she wrapped the
quilt tighter and peeked out the partially open study door.
She could hear sounds coming from the kitchen. It
sounded like someone humming a tuneless song. For some
odd reason it made her giggle.

Tiptoeing down the hall, she peeked into the

kitchen and her breath caught at the sight of Jake in his bare feet pouring coffee into a couple of mugs. His shirt was open, his chest bare. The sleeves of the blue button down were rolled up to his elbows and his hair was tousled. She watched him move about the kitchen, opening the refrigerator and pulling out the cream. She was amazed that he remembered she liked cream in her coffee. As she watched, she saw him glance toward the laundry alcove and heard the dryer ending its cycle. Curious, she watched him set down the coffee and walk over to the dryer. He opened the door and pulled out her dress, then her bra and panties. She felt herself blush as he held them up one by one, and draped them over his arm. He was looking around for something and, as she looked on, he found a clean towel and laid it on top of the washing machine. Carefully he laid out the bra and panties, arranging them almost artfully on the towel. Next he took a hangar from the rack and hung the dress, taking care to button the top button and smoothing the fabric. *Lucky for me it doesn't wrinkle easily,* she was thinking to herself when Jake reached for the iron and ironing board.

You've got to be kidding, she was stunned. As she watched, he set up the ironing board, and turned on the iron before removing the carefully hung dress from its hanger. Amazement turned to amusement as she watched him arrange the dress on the ironing board and prepare to iron it. He's good, she admitted to herself as she watched him iron her favorite dress. Perhaps I can hire him to do all my ironing? Finding her thoughts funny she had to stifle a giggle.

The smell of the coffee was getting to her. Deciding she could wait no longer, she snuck back down the hall a little way and then coughed loudly as she approached the kitchen, calling out his name softly.

"Hello? Jake?" She said in a voice she hoped was still a little sleepy, as if she had just woken up. "Coffee smells great," she was saying as she stepped into the kitchen.

To her surprise he had not hurried to put away the iron or hide the fact that he was using it.

"What on earth are you doing?" She asked incredulously.

"What does it look like, Sam?" He replied.

"It looks like you are ironing my dress—the one I was looking for I might add," she answered back with a faint blush as she hiked the quilt higher and tighter.

"Why would you need your dress? You look quite fetching in that quilt," he said with a smirk.

"Fetching? What kind of a word is that?" She shot back.

"An old fashioned word for someone who looks beautiful in the morning, wrapped in a quilt. I think you'd look good in a potato sack though," he said plainly.

Samantha just blushed deeper and could think of

nothing to say in retort.

"Your coffee is on the counter. I was going to bring it to you but the dryer went off and I wanted to get this taken care of first. If it's cold just pour a little more in it, there's plenty," he told her as he finished the body of the dress and rearranged it to iron the sleeves and collar.

"Why did you wash my dress? I don't remember spilling on it," she asked, savoring the flavor of the coffee as she did so.

"At some point one of us spilled something on it and I noticed it this morning so—I decided to let you sleep and take care of it myself."

"And why aren't you married?" She asked, only half teasing him,

Samantha knew the second she finished the sentence that it was the wrong thing to have said. Jake's smile faltered but stayed in place, the sparkle in his eyes dying quickly.

Turning away from her, ostensibly to pour another cup of coffee, he said "Was once for about ten days. It didn't work."

"I'm sorry—I apologize for that," she began.

"Why?" he asked, turning back to her, "Please don't apologize because of my reaction. There is no way you would have known, or should have known, and it's a natural question. It was something that happened a very long time ago and I'm...I should apologize to you. You caught me off guard."

Changing the subject, Samantha put a hand on his arm and smiled, "Do you cook as well as you iron? Or may I make you some breakfast?"

"I am a wonderful cook but my repertoire is limited so, I'd be honored to have you fix breakfast," he replied, setting his coffee cup down and beginning to button up his shirt.

She placed a hand on his and looked him in the eyes, "Don't do that on my account," she said softly, moving her hand to his bare chest.

"You look at me like that again and you'll be breakfast!" He answered with a wicked grin.

Samantha laughed and stepped backward, almost tripping on the hem of the quilt.

"I guess I better put something else on if I'm going to cook," she said, and before he could grab her, she spun away and went back down the hall toward her bedroom.

Ghosted

Jennie Elaine

The Ranger rattled like a dying breath. It was that loud kind of racket you got when the suspension was shot and your wallet limited your maintenance plan to just turning up the radio.

Jordan couldn't remember a time they'd had the volume below 32. Always old rock, since nothing else blocked out the sound enough, or felt *right*.

The setting Western sun turned the desert highway pink before them, a long stretch of nothing beyond his ringed fingers tapping on the wheel. Dog tags hung from the mirror, not his. The roar of wind mixed with the suspension and dad rock, blowing smoke back in from the passenger's side. He risked a glance over at Tristan, peeling his eyes from the road to take in his manic idiot riding shotgun.

Tristan's dark hair was pushed back, a messy wolf cut he did himself in hotel mirrors. It blew wildly around his face, not that he minded much. His torso was drowning in an oversized bomber jacket in spite of the heat, a black tank hiding his muscular chest while his dark jeans hugged those dangerously thick thighs. He was the kind of man who looked small at first glance. That was usually enough time for him to swing the first punch—Jordan knew from experience he had a mean right hook—and prove that assumption wrong. His boots were damn near falling apart, and he had enough piercings on his face to make a metal detector weep.

Jordan smiled in spite of himself, glancing back to the road.

"Yer bad for me."

"I know," Tristan replied, pulling his cigarette out of his mouth. With the hiss of burning flesh he put it out on the inside of his wrist, doubling over in silence before gasping in a breath through the pain and tossing the butt out the window. The wound healed over in less than a minute. His wild grin was infectious, his hazel eyes teasing when he turned to Jordan.

"But you love it."

Two hard kicks came to the back of Jordan's seat, *thump thump.*

"Remmick agrees with me," Jordan drawled, earning a laugh.

"Rem always agrees with you," Tristan pointed his fingers at him, "he's got a weak spot for that southern charm bullshit. He only takes your side 'cause he knows what you're packing under that large ass belt buckle–hey!"

Tristan laughed again as the kicking returned, this time against his seat. "I just call 'em like I see 'em, asshole!" He turned to wave an arm around in the empty back area of the extended cab, half leaning into Jordan. "Am I hitting you? Tell me if I'm hitting you."

"Leave him alone," Jordan smiled, "and get yer ass out of my face."

"You love my ass."

Jordan took one hand off the wheel to hit it, nearly sending Tristan into the back with a yelp and more laughter. His legs kicked wildly until he made his way back into the front, reaching for another cigarette in his pocket.

"Save it," Jordan advised, "we're almost there."

"I know," Tristan flicked open his favorite Zippo. "Why do you think I'm getting one more in? No smoking in a hospital."

Jordan rolled his eyes, turning back to the road.

"Not like they don't have bigger problems than second-hand smoke," Tristan grumbled as an afterthought, settling back into the sounds of wind, shot suspension, and another round of dad rock after the commercial break.

Jordan caught the briefest flash of blond hair and a smile in the rearview mirror, and then there were only the swinging dogtags hanging off of it. *He's not wrong*, that smile seemed to say.

Jordan tightened his hands on the wheel.

Especially if they've called us.

***

Mercy Central Hospital swallowed them in shadow when Jordan parked beneath its large brick mass. A

132

life-sized statue of some feminine religious icon stood between them and the front doors of what had to be the world's most remote medical center, located ten miles from the nearest town and just off a two lane highway. It was like someone had attempted to care enough to develop the land once upon a time, and yet only one plot sold.

"Middle of fucking nowhere," Tristan put out his cigarette on his arm again, flicking the butt out the window and reaching for the dogtags hanging from the mirror.

"*Everything* is the middle of nowhere out here," Jordan chided, stretching his arms high above his head as soon as his boots hit the cracked concrete. "There ain't a city anywhere near here, just small towns and desert for hours."

"Fucking Wyoming," Tristan swore, slamming his door and rounding to the truck bed. "I hate this state."

"You hate *every* state."

"Yeah," Tristan gave him, climbing up the wheel well to reach for his bag. It had a *San Diego Fire Department* logo across the front and looked like it was built to survive World War III. "But I especially hate any state with a desert or Appalachian hills. They've always got the fucked up jobs."

"Fair enough," Jordan shrugged his own bag across his shoulder, a long duffel that weighed half as much as he did.

"C'mon, Cowboy," Tristan jogged around to shove

his shoulder. "Let's get this job done and over and get the fuck out of here."

Jordan put his arm around his shoulders. "Just behave," he warned him, "the head nurse sounded real serious when we talked on the phone."

"You ever met a head nurse that didn't sound super serious all the time?" Tristan snorted. "I think it's in the job description. You should have met the one in charge of my last ward stay."

"Please don't say anything that could get you thrown in a mental ward?" Jordan practically begged his boyfriend.

"Babe, they called *us* to come clear out a ghost," Tristan dismissed him, "I don't think they'll admit me for being able to talk to invisible people."

"I sure hope not, Darlin'," Jordan sighed, letting go and leading them to the double doors.

He caught a glance of Rem's amused smile in the glass's reflection, standing behind and between them both.

"Hey," Tristan said, "stop me if you've heard this one; a cowboy, a ghost, and a psychic walk into a hospital..."

"I shoulda left your ass in Tempe," Jordan groaned.

***

"My nurses won't even go in the wing anymore," the head nurse, a portly middle aged woman with a no-nonsense haircut and a name like *Nancy* was saying, "refuse to move patients in there—anyone we wheel in starts to decline fast, even if they were a day from discharge just before. Shadows moving out of the corner of your eyes, lights flickering and completely going out."

"Sounds like a haunting alright," Tristan agreed, earning a wary look from Nancy.

She wasn't really sure about the punk-looking guy—security hadn't been, either—but she'd warmed right up to Jordan. It was hard not to, Tristan thought; he was just charming to the bone. Tall, with the comfortable muscles of someone who worked for them, inviting brown eyes with long lashes that sharpened his features and curled brown hair peeking out from under his hat. He always had a respectable amount of facial hair, just a bit past 5 o'clock shadow, that gave him a mature, trustworthy air. He was wearing his usual attire of dark country-boy jeans tucked into boots that had cost *way* more than you'd expect, and a simple blue button down with the sleeves rolled up to show off his driver's tan.

He looked like the kind of guy you'd trust to help you with car troubles in the dead of night on the side of an empty highway. That thick southern accent and the constantly peppered in '*yes ma'am's*' didn't hurt, either.

"It's gotten out of hand," Nancy continued, looking back to Jordan as they turned a corner to face a set of closed double doors halfway down the hallway. "Thank you for coming all the way out here. My sister, Trisha, works in

Tallahassee. Referred me after you helped them with some properties that way last year.”

“Yes ma’am,” Jordan confirmed. “The office building renovations. I remember.”

“She said there were three of you,” Nancy frowned, stopping a healthy distance away from the closed doors.

“There are,” Tristan said, “Rem got a little pinned down in California. He’s here in spirit, though.”

The look Jordan gave him over Nancy’s shoulder could have curdled milk. He only flashed him a wicked smile.

“We can handle it,” Jordan reassured her, “is this the wing?”

“It’s empty right now. Per your request. My girls were thrilled to hear no one had to work it tonight.”

Jordan moved towards the doors, reaching out with an open palm to place it against the light wood. He closed his eyes, feeling the room beyond through touch. “We moved the patients out last night,” Nancy continued, but neither were paying attention to her now. Tristan watched Jordan’s face in profile as the smile on his lips slipped away into something more serious. “How long do you think this will take?”

“Not sure yet,” Jordan said, pulling his hand back and turning to her with a serious expression. “You were right to call us, though. We’ll do everything we can to clean house.”

Tristan read his expression well enough. "You might wanna head back to the nurses station," he advised her, stepping up to the doors. "We'll be back when it's finished."

"Right," she looked worried, then schooled her expression, stood up straighter, and turned back towards the front. "Good luck, boys."

They waited until she was out of sight and hearing range before Tristan turned to Jordan, eyebrow raised.

"Whatever it is," the cowboy drawled, "it ain't good."

Tristan turned, grabbing the metal handle and pushing the door in. "Yeah? We're better."

They stepped into a dim hospital wing beyond. It was primarily used for overnight patients, a straight hall with linoleum floors, a small empty nurses station on the right, and patient room doors on the left. The air felt instantly heavier, like a blanket muffling the soft ambient noises of the hospital around them.

"You weren't kidding," Tristan stepped forward first, walking just past the station to peer down the length of the hall. "The air feels awful here."

"What do you see?" Jordan asked, a few steps behind.

"Nothing, yet."

Tristan took a breath, setting his bag down and peering down the length of the hall. At the far end, despite having the same lights as the rest of the space, the light seemed... dimmer. Like deep water instead of air, a darkness caused only by perception.

He reached down into his bag, grabbed a small wax seal, and snapped it in half. The hall echoed with it, a small pulse of energy coming from the wax in his hands. *His* energy, placed there with the help of Jordan's skill in enchanted objects.

Bait.

He waited. The sudden spike of energy released was a dinner bell to anything nearby. Nothing moved at the end of the hall for a long moment, but the hair on the back of Tristan's neck raised, instincts telling him to keep his eyes there.

Then, movement. A shadow behind a broken ceiling tile shifted, barely noticeable at first. Then again, more. The darkness moved with purpose then, the size of an average man minus the details or face clinging to the ceiling on lengthened arms and legs.

Tristan leaned back on his heels, clicking his tongue bar against his teeth. "Oh, you fuckers have been chasin' me for a *long* time," he laughed at the spindly dark stain that crawled down from the ceiling, no fear in his eyes. On silent haunches it dropped down only ten feet away. His eyes lit up with a wild spark, an electric pressure spilling from him like water pushing through a swelling dam.

"Shadowman."

They were shades of spirits, proof that even terrible people could die and still carry on. They lost all form, and without a mouth to speak or fists to hit with, they turned to syphoning away the energy of the living to fill their need for cruelty. Left to their own devices they just kept feeding and feeding, never stopping. The only way to evict them was a harsh infusion of positive energy, drowning them out until they simply *ceased.*

It wasn't their first rodeo dealing with one.

"You want me?" The medium shouted over the scream of fluorescent lights that grew brighter and brighter in his vicinity, the fold of his energy licking them to life. He held his hand before him, Rem's dogtags dangling from them like a crucifix, curling his painted fingers at the shadowman.

"Come and get me."

Raw manic energy. It was both what Tristan *was,* and his specialty. Darkness gathered behind the shadow, the corridor growing long, endless, and then it was surging forward, arms outstretched to grab Tristan and take from him everything he had to give.

A lighthouse in a dark sea of energy, many mediums like Tristan attracted things from the other world like a beacon, unable to hide their shine or do anything with the spiritual energy within them, a veritable buffet for monsters that go bump in the night.

Tristan was not one of those mediums.

The shadowman clashed with a solid wall of will, throwing its hand aside and pushing its momentum back upon it. The shadowman receded back into the corridor without choice, silent to the ears but loud to the senses. Anger and malice scraped their minds like claws, rage at being pushed away from such a well of power it craved.

Jordan shook it off, familiar with the vitriol of shadow beings. In the time Tristan had drawn the shadow's attention he'd dropped his duffel bag, thrown back the zipper, and pulled from the recesses an unearthed fencepost, weathered and worn.

It was nothing more than a blunt pole to the naked eye, grey with age and nicked all to heaven and back. But to Jordan, it was the cornerpost of home.

Through his hands he felt the call of spring breezes chasing winter from the ranch, the labor his great grandfather had put into erecting their homestead, and the love of his grandmother every year that she'd marked his changed height with a new chiseled line against the post.

Home was a power all its own, and it made an even more powerful weapon when put in the hands of a psychometrist who could wield it.

Tristan lashed out at the shadow again like a whip, laughing on the high of releasing so much power and pushing it further away. "Kick him down, babe," he called to Jordan, who was already running around him. Swinging the post underhanded like a golf club.

The shadow man, to him, wasn't a visible thing so much as it was a feeling of something taking up space where it shouldn't. The impossibility of it, the raw, disgusting negative energy that rolled around its form and settled into the walls was everything his fence post from home wasn't. Unwanted. Impure.

Even if he couldn't see it, you didn't have to be precise when you were swinging a giant piece of wood.

The post collided with the shadowman, hitting its side with the spiritual equivalent of sparks where the beam touched it. It silently screamed in Jordan's mind, attempting to right itself and lunge for him, but Tristan was faster.

Before it could right itself and reach Jordan another wave from Tristan's near infinite well surged over it, flattening it down on the ground. Sensing the center of negative energy, Jordan raised the post like he meant to stake it into the ground, gathered his strength, and plunged it into the shadowman's chest.

He began to pull on the emotions of home from the post, amplifying and adding to its life over and over and sending it down into the creature. Tristan, as he'd done countless times before, raised his hand with the dogtags in it and poured his energy into them, giving Rem access to his stores of power the shadow had so coveted.

Jordan kept pushing down, the end of the post now

less than a foot off the floor, beads of sweat falling from his brow with the effort. In moments a second set of hands joined his, large and tan, giving the attack extra strength.

Rem was gritting his teeth in effort the same way he had done so in life, blond eyebrows furrowed in concentration, his muscles bulging as if he had a body to strain. Jordan didn't risk looking at him fully and losing sight of his goal, but those hands pushed down with his as they fought through the shadowman's negative form inch by inch, a true group effort, until at last the post jolted and slammed into the floor.

Shadows pulled away from the ground, oozing into the air and disappearing like ash in the wind. The lights returned to normal, the hall quiet.

Tristan whooped behind them, laughing openly. "Not today, you shadow-dicked assholes!" He punched the air, Rem's dogtags swinging haplessly in his fist. "Score zero for you fucks and 24 for me!"

Jordan pushed off his hat to wipe his brow, leaning heavily on the post for support. "You act like you did any of the hard work," he joked, turning to his right at last to see the third man standing there.

Rem. His heart ached as it always did in the rare moments when he got to view him fully. He was tall, pushing over six feet of chiseled muscle and broad shoulders. His blonde hair was stained with grey ash, his white undershirt smeared with sooted fingerprints. His lower half was partially dressed in a pair of fireman's turnout pants held in place by suspenders, and the equivalent boots to match. He was smiling softly at Jordan, one he'd seen a thousand times before he'd died.

Good job, that smile said. Jordan gave him one in return.

"Come on," Tristan's voice called through the silent wing, "let's go back outside, I could really use a smoke."

Rem's smile slipped away at the same time Jordan's did. In the silent wing.

Too silent, still.

"Tristan, hold on," Jordan called over his shoulder, reaching to the nearest wall. Beneath the paint the cool drywall pulled at him the same way the door had before they'd entered, low and menacing.

"Something ain't right," he said, at the same time he felt a sharp pull on his arm, and the feeling of a sea breeze that only came from one person when they touched him.

Rem. He turned his direction, but he didn't see Rem at all. He didn't see anything, but he felt what occupied the space just behind him all the same.

Something dark, and menacing, a black shape that was barely outlined in his eye. Something different from the shadowman. Something worse.

I hate the states with a desert in them, Tristan had complained, *they always got the fucked up jobs.*

Because the chances of running into some inhuman spirit in the desert was higher. The land was alive, a thrumming hub of energy far louder than other parts of the country.

It was a battery in its own right, one that drew a different kind of spiritual being to feed off of it, things that were older and more powerful. Things that could wield the energy of the land to their bidding.

And whatever was standing to the side of him was one of those things.

"Jordan!" Tristan shouted, the lights flickering violently overhead, and in the darkness, in spite of his lack of spiritual sight, Jordan saw what was before him.

He had no words.

It reached out for him, long, inhuman fingers reaching, stretching, *yearning*—

He tried to move away, but he couldn't. He couldn't. His feet wouldn't move, stuck in place like quicksand beneath the oppressive weight of fear. The hand came closer, brushing the air in front of his chest, and with it came the deep, painful cold of despair, of empty winter nights, of hollow horrors deep in caverns and nightmares you couldn't shake–

Tristan slammed into him like a freight train. Jordan went sprawling on the floor, snapping immediately from the psychic onslaught just in time to see the wide eyes of his boyfriend, fear written on his expression, the moment he replaced where Jordan had been standing and was grabbed instead.

"*Tristan!*" He shouted over his boyfriend's strangled cry. The thing was there one moment in the dark, gone the next in the light, and with each blink of the fluorescents Jordan watched it raise Tristan up by the chest, higher, higher, his feet kicking listlessly beneath him.

Move! His mind screamed, and then he was up and moving, grabbing the post from the floor beside him. The being had moved to the middle of the room in the space between light flickers, its back to him, Tristan held above its head. The wild electricity that surrounded his boyfriend moved in chaos and without focus, like water emptying down a drain. A drain leading right to the being.

Jordan kneeled, setting up his post at a steep angle, and with a sharp cry of effort snapped through another onslaught of terror and fear to flare his post's vibrancy to life and slam it like a bettering ram into the small of the being's back.

It was like driving into a brick wall with his truck. The crash back damn near threw him from his feet, and only sheer will of strength in his legs kept him upright, kept him pushing. Just as he had moments before Rem's hands joined his, pouring everything he had to give into the attack and keeping it going.

But something wasn't right.

Rem flickered—there one heartbeat, gone the next, and then back again—fighting to stay corporeal even as Tristan's well of energy was drained from him. Despair was written on his silent features, and each new flash of his form changed for the worse. His hair singed away, blood began to leak down his head from the beam that had knocked him prone. His skin changed from tan, to red, to dark black, his clothes burning away until he looked like a shadowman himself, dark and faceless, only a stain in human form.

Tristan doesn't have enough energy for him to borrow, Jordan realised with alarm, he doesn't have enough left, *I can't let the shadowman take it all, I can't, I have to, I have to–!*

The beam grew suddenly heavy, the second pair of hands pushing it forward falling away completely. Rem was gone, cut off from Tristan's energy without enough to stay corporeal.

"*Tristan!*" Jordan shouted, seeing the whites of his boyfriend's eyes when they rolled back, his head lolling back. "Tristan!"

He pushed with his feet, scraped the floor, damn near ran in place, but it was no use. The post didn't move, didn't do *anything*. Tristan's feet stopped kicking, his breathing labored, shallow, his head lolling back.

This thing was going to *eat* him. And then, when it was done, it was going to turn on Jordan. And there was nothing he could do to stop it. Not on his own.

The fluorescent lights overhead suddenly lit brighter and brighter, the whiteness blinding, until one by one they exploded in a shower of sparks down the hallway. The pole's weight lifted considerably, Rem standing beside him again, eyes blazing with determination, pulling his strength from the lights until they'd exploded.

The notches in the post lit up a bright green glow as Rem poured everything he had into the post, a silent scream on his lips. Jordan joined with everything *he* had, one last push, the post pulsing energy into the being faster and faster, the winds over the fields, the love of his family, the pure well of all that was good, all that was *loved*–

With the force of a small explosion the being dissipated, burning from within in agony. A scream like nails in a garbage disposal rang out from its lips, dropping Tristan like dead weight onto the floor. Jordan slipped, falling, Rem catching his arm while the post hit the ground, the being chasing itself in place, spinning, clawing at its back and chest to no avail, cracks splitting across its unholy flesh peeling out the green light of their will, of their love for Tristan.

And then, it was gone.

The air returned. The lights of the nurses station, untouched by Rem, returned to life. Tristan didn't move.

Jordan scrambled to him, his hat discarded somewhere on the floor. He grabbed Tristan and pulled him to his chest just as his eyes opened, a deep gasp pulling air into his lungs.

Jordan turned him to let him cough, the light returning to his eyes, pinkness filling out his cheeks.

"Don't you *ever* do that to me again!" Jordan shouted, pulling Tristan against his chest in a tight, desperate hug. He pressed his nose into the shorter man's neck, squeezing his eyes shut.

"I thought I'd lost you, too," he whispered, and Tristan's heart felt like it was made of lead.

Over his shoulder Tristan could see Rem kneeling beside Jordan, his hand on his back, his mouth in a tight, worried line. It didn't take much imagination to know what Jordan was thinking about.

I thought I'd lost you, too.

Tristan's arms came around to hug Jordan, holding him as tight as he could manage.

"I'm sorry, babe," he breathed, "I'm here. I'm alive. I'm sorry."

Rem brushed some hair from Tristan's face, the feeling a cold whisper on his hot skin.

"I'm okay," he reassured him next, reaching out to him. "I'm okay."

The three of them sat on the floor together for a long time, the now silent hospital wing granting them their privacy, if only for a moment. Two beating hearts, and one long since stilled, meeting as one in the wake of near tragedy.

"I'm sorry," Tristan whispered again.

***

The car ride from Mercy Central was as quiet as their shitty Ranger would allow. The radio had turned itself off again, leaving only the sound of wind and the loud ass suspension for them to listen to.

Jordan hadn't taken his hand out of Tristan's the entire ride, and Tristan hadn't pulled away, even when his fingers went numb. The back seat looked empty, save for the folding seats, but Tristan kept Rem's dogtags around his chest, and he could feel him in the space.

Jordan found them some rundown single-floor motel outside the other side of the saddest town Tristan had ever seen. It wasn't until he parked next to the small office building and killed the engine that he let go of his hand.

"I'll go pay," Jordan said, brushing a thumb along Tristan's jaw. "Wait here for me, Darlin'?"

"I'll be here," he promised. Jordan still let his eyes linger on him for a long minute before he got out the driver's side and disappeared through the wooden door, windchimes clinking in his wake.

Tristan ran a hand through his hair with a long exhale, slipping out his own door to lean against the side of the truck and light up a cigarette.

For my wildfire, read the inscription on his Zippo,

and he ran his thumb over the words caught by the neon vacancy sign. The truck shifted slightly as another body seemed to join him, blonde hair and tan skin visible just out of the corner of his eye.

Tristan took a long drag off of his cigarette. "I know what you'd say," he told Rem, breathing smoke out with each word. "And you're right. I'm not a hero. That was always you."

Rem, as always, was silent. Tristan continued.

"It's why you got out of high school and ran straight to the military. A medic. Then you came back and ran right into being a firefighter. And then you ran right into a burning building and never came back out."

He took another drag from his cigarette, trying to pull his thoughts together. Tears threatened his eyes. He looked down to hide behind a curtain of his hair. "And then, when we broke after losing you, you ran right back to us. I'm not a hero. I'm a selfish, self-destructive ass and when that thing went after Jordan I didn't...I couldn't...I couldn't be a hero. I could only be me."

He felt the light brush of a hand pushing back his hair and he turned to face Rem head on. He'd expected condemnation, even disappointment on his features, but his handsome face was relaxed. Understanding.

I know, his bright blue eyes said, *and I'll always be there for you when you are.*

It was something he'd said to him a thousand times

before. They'd met in school when Tristan had nearly set himself and half a home economics class on fire fucking around with the stove. Rem had been the one to put him out with the extinguisher, and that had set the tone of their friendship, and eventual relationship.

No matter what chaos Tristan suffered unto himself, Rem was there to pull him out. Even when he left for the military and Tristan had met Jordan, Rem had taken one look at his stupid boyfriend and the dark mental pit he'd put himself in over his feelings for another man and just smiled before welcoming said man into the fold.

Rem had always just been good at being *good*...at always being there for him. And he'd told him as much a thousand times. Even tonight, he'd not given up on him.

Tristan closed his eyes. "Thank you. I'm sorry. I miss you, but I ain't planning to join you any time soon, either. I promise."

He felt knuckles lightly tapping his forehead. *You better not*, he could imagine him saying.

Tristan snorted. "Naw," he opened his eyes again, "someone's gotta keep corrupting our bleeding-heart cowboy."

A third weight leaned against the truck on his other side, Jordan sighing. He wrapped one large arm around Tristan, pulling his back to his chest.

"Yer so fucking bad for me," he grumbled, burying a kiss on his neck.

Tristan laughed, putting the cigarette out on the ground this time. It would take a while to replenish his energy, and all the perks that came with it, like faster healing. "You love me, though."

"I love both of you," he argued, "but right now Rem is winning."

Tristan whined while Rem's spirit hit his fist in the air in silent celebration. Jordan cracked a smile, holding up the room key dangling from a plastic tag.

"*He's a literal ghost*," Tristan argued.

"What's not to love about that? He's quiet."

"I'm quiet!" Tristan argued loudly.

"Thoughtful."

"Oh I've got so many thoughts."

"That's not what that means—*and* he helped me save your life tonight."

"Only after I saved yours!" He tried to wriggle free from his hold to no avail. Jordan laughed, reaching down to scoop up his legs and carry him bridal style towards their hotel door.

"Yer such a dumbass," Jordan laughed, letting him kick and fight the air without actual bite.

Rem stayed behind by the truck, feeling the pull of his boyfriends walk away from him. He turned to look up at the sky, a small smile on his face.

I can't fix the car, he thought to himself, feeling his energy slip away to the quiet spaces he inhabited when

Tristan wasn't near. *But I will do anything else for them.*

Even fight the afterlife. Even travel the country fighting ghosts as Tristan had always wanted to do.

The hotel door closed around Jordan and Tristan's play fighting, Rem disappearing from sight, but following them in.

Watcher

LeAnne Keely

Lucia couldn't shake the feeling of being watched. It was a creeping, whole-body tingle that she couldn't mistake for anything else in the world. She'd felt it on patrol, on the battlefield, and on occasion here in her adopted home of Paradise.

She felt suddenly naked without her mech, but her Hellhound, Gjallar, was over a mile away, deep in the hangar of the Gambit.

You've gone soft.

She made a conscious effort not to pick up her pace, wandering nonchalantly through the open air market of Brine Street. This part of town was seedy, but far less so than it had been a year ago. She and Liam, along with some of their allies, had done a great deal to clean up the streets, but their activities had made them plenty of enemies.

She took stock of herself as she moved between the stalls. Her long, red, nearly floor length skirt covered the tops of her supple gray leather riding boots, and the polished steel handles of the twin daggers she kept there, her flowy gray blouse disguised ballistic armor - a present from Liam's own shop - and twin 9mm handguns resting securely in armpit holsters beneath her tan, cropped jacket.

All told she was well armed, even discounting her considerable hand-to-hand skills. But that could only take her so far, and only if she knew what she was up against. She meandered towards an alley that connected the clothing section of the market to Coral Street, where the firearms vendors gathered. The alley wasn't the most open route, in fact it was cramped and seldom used except by vendors moving merchandise. Anyone following her would be easily spotted.

She grabbed for her cellphone as she walked, typing out a quick message to her Captain.

[[Sir - spot of trouble. I'm being tailed, unknown who or how many. At Coral St. Market.]]

She sent the text off just as she slipped into the alley, her shoes padding softly over old stone. Shadows fell over her as she crossed between towering brownstones on either side. Her senses were on high alert, if someone wanted to accost her they'd be hard pressed to find a more suitable spot for an ambush. She didn't vary her pace, but was strung tighter than a violin waiting for an impact.

She found herself passing back into the light as she left the alley behind. A shiver ran down her spine and she pretended to take a look at the first stall she found. The man's wares were fine, but her true focus was the alley behind her.

It was... empty?

Lucia couldn't help but shake her head. Was she going crazy? Certainly not. Years of military training screamed at her that something, something was on her tail. But her eyes, desperate to find something out of place, came up short. She shook her head and pulled her phone out again.

[[Nevermind, I think. Headed back to the Gambit.]]

"Easy now."

A voice from behind made her blood run cold, she would know it anywhere. Phone in hand her whole body tensed as she shifted gears from alert to full-blown fight or flight mode. Lucia took another glance across the rooftops nearby, then scanned the crowd. He wouldn't have approached her alone.

"Reggie," she managed past gritted teeth.

She couldn't see him, but the tall, lanky bastard had put a bullet in her once, and that wasn't the kind of thing you tended to forget. He'd been a member of Wild Gambit back then, and so had... Well, best not to dwell on old wounds at the moment. She could picture him without turning. 6'4" and a wiry one-eighty-ish he was fast as hell and a damn good shot. He'd be wearing a vest, certainly, but he was too cocky for much else.

She glanced about the crowded area, wishing she had confidence he wouldn't shoot with all these innocent bystanders around.

But she knew better.

Maybe if she could just–

"Pretty shirt you've got on, Sarge."

Lucia's eyes flicked downward and she noted not one but two red dots trained on her chest. A defeated sigh left her lips.

"Where is she?"

"Waiting for you," Reggie drawled. "You gonna make this harder than it has to be?"

A flash of silk and sweat, dark red wine and sultry laughter pulled her focus for a moment.

"No," she managed past her tightening throat.

She made a show of straightening her back, looking around a moment, and adjusting the hem of her shirt.

"Good, I'd hate to make a scene, or a mess out of those clothes of yours."

A small chirp from the phone still in her hands made her wince, it was unmistakable that she'd just sent a message.

"Oh, that was a bad choice, Lucia."

She heard a rustle of fabric and the beginning of

the impact on the back of her head before falling into darkness.

Lucia woke to darkness as well, though the soft fabric wrapped around her eyes likely had more to do with that. Her head hurt like...well like she'd been pistol-whipped by a man with a grudge.

Pushing past the pain, she took in as much information as she could. Her knives were gone, ditto the pistols, but she had her ballistic vest on still. She could feel the chair she was tied to was quite fine, and judging from the smells of melting wax and slowly warming wine she was in a restaurant or bar.

Of course, one other scent rose above the others. Warm sugar and red wine married into an unmistakable allure. Boucheron, Destiny Boucheron's signature perfume and one of the many sources of income the heiress enjoyed.

"Lucia," her host's word purred softly, stoking coals that no amount of time or distance could cool. "Lucia, you've been avoiding me, my love."

She could hear the pout in Destiny's voice.

Strong fingers brush her cheeks, making her jump. She struggled against the chair, the wood creaking as the fabric binding her wrists tugged against it.

"Settle down," Destiny whispered in her ear and Lucia suppressed a shiver of a different kind.

Lucia stilled automatically, even her breath catching.

"Good girl."

Heat burned in her cheeks, but she remained silent as the silk scarf covering her eyes was untied and unwrapped.

The room was fairly dark, so her eyes didn't take much time to adjust. They were indeed in a restaurant, though one she didn't recognize. Dark wood and plush red cushions adorned everything and small, intimate tables and booths filled the place. There was a bar as well, rows and rows of crystal glasses and bottles of fancy booze.

And all of it empty.

The table in front of her had a spotless white tablecloth, gold-rimmed porcelain dishes, and a small, flickering candle. There was no food, not yet, but an open bottle of Porto Kelviche—the dark, velvety red that she'd always favored—set between them. Destiny's cup was already half drained, with deep purple lipstick staining the rim, where Lucia's was still empty.

"Are you going to untie my hands," Lucian raised an eyebrow. "Or am I just going to watch you—"

"Would you like to just watch," Destiny interrupted, cutting Lucia's sentence short. "You used to like that, if I recall."

Lucia's tongue was lead, and her throat was closing. Her heartbeat thudded behind her vest and she felt her inner thighs growing hotter and hotter.

Damn this woman.

She chose instead to examine her lover-to-enemy ex. She sported the same pixie-curl combination she always had, though her hair was black now, and not the blonde she'd seen last. She was 5'7", and most people would probably describe her as on the plump side of curvy. Her features were youthful, and not a single blemish touched her barely-tan complexion. Tonight she was wearing a black satin dress shirt and - Lucia assumed - trousers and dress shoes. A shoulder holster sat in open view and within it a custom .475 Black Cat revolver.

"I see you kept your anniversary present," Lucia quipped, trying to shift momentum as she studied her surroundings more closely.

"How's your head."

It wasn't spoken as a question, not really, but the piercing emerald eyes across the table demanded an answer regardless.

"It hurts," she answered honestly. "I'm probably concussed."

Destiny's eyes hardened in a way that sent shivers down her spine. She knew this look. Sweat broke out at the base of her neck but dammit if it wasn't making her squirm too.

"Devisto tre Reggie," the woman snapped , her eyes looking over Lucia's shoulder.

"Destiny, we-"

The other woman held up a single finger and Lucia snapped shut her mouth.

Moments later she heard a door open, shut, then reopen again. Two, no three pairs of footsteps approached from behind her. Her nerves frayed until the three men stepped into view beside the table. Reggie was smiling, relaxed, and flanked by two men business casual.

"I gave you very specific instructions, did I not?"

To most, her question seemed light, innocent even, but Lucia knew better

"And Reggie delivers," he smirked at Lucia. "Right, boss?"

Poor bastard.

Lucia flinched as Destiny drew the pistol in a fraction of a second. A roaring bang and several inches of fire left the gun barrel and a two-inch hole ripped open in the middle of Reggie's right lung.

Blood splattered the side of Lucia's face as she grimaced as Reggie's face went through shock and into terror in mere moments. He dropped to his knees and then to the floor where he lay on his back rasping and writhing and clutching his chest in pain.

The two men bent to retrieve the dying man, but stopped when Destiny waved them away.

"Leave him," Destiny's eyes flashed again, her face as calm and collected as a porcelain doll's, and her eyes blazing with anger.

"Out."

She flicked her eyes to Lucia, sending lightning through her body.

"She likes to watch."

Destiny held smoldering eye contact with her as the two goons left swiftly and silently.

Lucia felt herself chewing her lower lip, felt her nipples harden against the inside of her ballistic vest.

Something is fucking wrong with you.

She thought back to their younger days, first with the Yal-tan Special Forces and then, later, as mercenaries. Lucia had eventually grown tired of killing for money instead of principles.

Destiny had no such issue.

The woman's family were nobility in Yel-tan before the revolution, and like the rest of the aristocracy, she'd seen all of them hanged one by one before. She was the de facto head of what remained of Yel-tan's loyalists—mostly battle-tested soldiers and partisans—by the time she was twenty, and she'd built it into an empire in the shadows of her former nation.

Lucia's mind derailed further when she was finally able to break away from Destiny's eyes. She found herself drawn down Destiny's well-angled chin, to her shoulders and the tantalizing glimpses of pink and black lace poking out of her dress shirt just so. The first two buttons were already undone, and drawing the weapon seemed to have unbuttoned a third.

"Hungry?"

Lucia snapped her eyes upward again, red burning in her face as she tried to conceal that she was softly grinding her thighs together under the table to keep from blurting out anything... stupid.

"Lucia, Jester," She stood suddenly, clearly enjoying the reaction she got from using Lucia's old call sign. "I asked if you were hungry."

She gulped as the woman stalked around the table like a panther, ignoring the dying man beside them. She stepped up to Lucia's chair and reached out a hand, cupping her chin gently.

"And you know my pet peeve, don't you baby?"

The grip tightened and Lucia felt her face jerked upward until she couldn't help but meet those green eyes.

"I like to be answered, when I ask a question," her eyes were hungry again. "Don't I?"

"Yes," she choked out.

"Yes, you know my pet peeve? Yes, you're hungry?"

Lucia ground her teeth.

In a blink the pistol was back out, this time the still warm tip of the barrel was pressed against Lucia's temple.

"Be specific."

Lucia whimpered, not with fear but with a curling mixture of shame and lust.

"I'm hungry, Destiny," she gulped, her mouth suddenly dry. "I'm very hungry."

Destiny laughed, then pulled back the pistol. She popped open the wheel and pulled out the spent casing, and 2 other cartridges as well, then gave it a spin and popped it back in.

"Destiny, what are you-"

"You used to love this game baby."

She pulled her shirt hard, the remaining button popping off to expose a lacey, barely-there bra and the evidence of years of hard living. She was fit, but thick like a gymnast. Her skin was marred by scars from guns and knives and burns. Most, Lucia knew the story.

There were a few new ones.

"Boys first," she turned the gun toward Reggie and pulled the trigger.

Another gunshot ripped into the man, his thigh this time and he groaned in pain.

"Well would you look at that," Destiny's smile was a bit too wide. "Just two left I suppose."

"Untie me."

"Was that a question? It should've been, right?"

"Yes, sorry," Lucian shivered. "Will you untie me, please?"

"Because you're hungry."

Lucia nodded.

Her voice caught in her throat when Destiny put

the gun to her temple again.

"I love you baby."

click

Lucia's chest swelled and her core quivered at the sound, and it damn near pushed her over the edge.

Destiny's lips captured hers, her tongue forcing past Lucia's lips and her free hand buried in Lucia's hair. The last few walls Lucia was maintaining crumbled immediately. Now, her struggles against the bindings were not to escape, but from desire alone.

"Fuck me."

"That's supposed to be a question."

Lucia groaned as Destiny danced out of range. She watched the woman put the gun under her own chin, then smile, wink, and pull the trigger.

click

Lucia let out the breath she'd only just begun to hold.

"Looks like we're both lucky."

Destiny stepped back and removed what was left of her shirt, revealing strong arms and the dark blue ritual tattoos of her people on her left arm. She set the revolver on the table and picked up her wine glass, content to take a sip while Lucia tried hard not to whimper with desire.

You've fought and killed and bled on battlefields dammit, get yourself togeth-

Destiny stepped forward and grabbed Lucia's chin

again, squeezing it hard enough to force her mouth open, then poured in enough red wine that some overflowed from the corners of her mouth. It was room temperature and heady, just barely sweet and deeply oaked it was sinfully soft on her tongue and lips. Lucia gulped it greedily, her body shaking as Destiny's free hand reached between her legs and lifted her skirt up until it was bunched in her lap.

Deft fingers slipped past the thin fabric of her underwear and Lucia saw Destiny smirk as she felt how wet she was.

"Well you're not fooling anyone," she teased, plunging two fingers inside all the way to the third knuckle. "You missed me, baby."

"Wh-wh-why am I here, Destiny," Lucia managed, trying hard to keep her eyes from rolling as Destiny's palm pressed against her clit, and her fingers crooked and rubbed against her g-spot.

"Does there have to be a reason," Destiny pretended, poorly, to be shocked.

"There's always a reason," Lucia said more firmly, gasping a little as Destiny removed her fingers. "You stopped needing me for anything other than a job years ago and we both know it."

"Oh that's not true, baby," Destiny reached past Lucia only to reveal one of her own daggers.

Lucia gripped the armrests of her chair, heart

pounding hard enough she could feel in her now empty—now aching—core.

The dagger had some of her interest, certainly, but the long thick print against Destiny's slacks had her attention.

"Oh you are hungry," Destiny laughed.

She spun the dagger in her hand, then slammed it point first into the armrest, just between Lucia's first and second fingers. The steel edge grazed her skin enough to draw a line of flame that immediately began to weep scarlet.

"Two for flinching," Destiny's tone grew serious again.

Lucia braced herself as the woman kicked the legs of the chair, spinning her so she faced away from the table. She undid her belt, the silver buckle flashing in the candlelight, then slowly, teasingly, under the button and pulled down her zipper.

"Fuck," Lucia breathed, unintentionally aloud.

Lucia's face blazed as her ex's seven thick inches of cock embraced the freedom of the open air. She sidled forward, closing to just a foot or so away from Lucia.

"Open up."

Lucia set her jaw, doing her best to look unimpressed.

A smack burned across her face, the sound echoing across the room and Lucia saw stars a moment, shaking her head to recover.

"Open up."

Lucia's façade faded, she could no longer pretend she had any control in this situation—or that she wanted any. Instead she made direct eye contact and opened her mouth, letting her jaw hang slack.

"Reach for it," Destiny's voice was huskier with every word.

And every word sent pulses of longing deep inside of Lucia.

She obediently leaned forward as far as she could, desperate for a taste, only to find she could quite reach. With increasing desperation she strained against her bonds, half angry and half wild at the growing grin on Destiny's face.

"Beg for–"

"Please, fuck my face."

Another smile, this time accompanied by a strong step forward. Lucia didn't wait for an invitation. She dragged her tongue up the length of Destiny's shaft and then, when she reached the tip, shoved it down her throat. Her body resisted, her throat fighting the effort, the strain, but she forced her way down until her lips pressed Destiny's body. She could feel every heartbeat in the woman's cock, feel the veins pushing against her throat and the rising need to breathe. She swirled her tongue, eliciting and a twitch from Destiny.

Now it was Lucia's turn to smirk, as well as she could with her throat full.

She moved to withdraw only to feel Destiny's hand grab the back of her head. The woman was careful to avoid her existing injury, but with a sharp clench into Lucia's hair made it clear who would decide when she could breathe again.

"Not yet."

Lucia felt her slowly, painfully, begin to drag her head back. Tears sprang into her eyes and the edges of her vision started to grow fuzzy and with every second she got closer and closer to her own climax.

With another yank, hard enough to snap her head back, Destiny popped free. Lucia sucked in air and coughed, her lungs burning and her chest on fire as thin ribbons of saliva connected them.

"More?"

"More."

She closed her eyes in ecstasy as Destiny fucked her face, ramming her dick into Lucia's throat over and over, pushing her to the brink of passing out before granting her breath again. Lucia could've cum from this alone, she'd done so before, but every time she was about to hit the precipice Destiny would pull out.

Finally, after nearly blacking out yet again, she growled and twisted her head away before glaring upward.

"Untie me."

This time there was no pushback.

Destiny grabbed the knife and slashed through her bonds, gripping her blouse with her free hand and yanking Lucia to her feet.

The knife found her throat and she dared not speak. Instead, she allowed Destiny to turn her around until she faced the bloodstained table. A glance down at Reggie confirmed the poor bastard was still alive–if only just.

Destiny let out a sharp whistle, one hand still holding the knife and the other roughly tearing open Lucia's blouse.

One of the bodyguards stepped into the room, causing Lucia to flush with embarrassment.

"Clear the table, leave the bottle."

The man approached wordlessly, picked up the dishes without making eye contact with either of them, and started to walk away.

"Tell her she's beautiful."

The man paused, then half-turned.

"You're very beautiful."

"Tell her she's sexy."

Lucia moaned as the woman gripped her breast firmly, rolling her nipple between two fingers.

"You're very sexy, ma'am."

"Now get the fuck out."

He scurried back out of the room and the second he

was gone Lucia felt herself slammed down onto the table. The impact knocked the wind out of her. Down came the knife, this time pinning the collar of her leather jacket to the table. She felt her skirt hiked up, and her panties torn to the side.

"Des-," her voice stuttered into a long groan and the woman entered her, burying her womanhood to the hilt.

Lucia hadn't been stretched this wide in a very long time, but the feeling was delicious. Again and again Destiny rammed into her, slamming hard enough she knew she'd have bruises on her thighs from the table's edge. Her pleasure built like a rising tide, she could feel herself vibrating with the need to release, but something held her back. She lost track of time, of everything except the relentless pounding and the increasingly ragged breathing of the woman behind her.

"Cum for me," Destiny managed through grit teeth.

Lucia was close, but not there yet, she opened her eyes, tried to focus, and found herself staring at the silver gun still atop the table.

You're fucking broken.

She snaked a hand out, grabbed it and shoved it backwards toward Destiny. The woman caught it before it slid off the table, her laughter dark and thrilling. Lucia heard the wheel pop open, then saw a single bullet placed in front of her on the table.

One left.

The wheel spun behind her and the barrel pressed against her side, almost making her cum on the spot. She tried to speak but the pounding resumed, this time it felt like only seconds before she was racing unstoppable toward a cliff's edge.

"N-now," she gasped, unable to control it.

A roaring bang and sudden pain streaked across her side, accompanied by an impact like a sledgehammer. Her pussy clenched uncontrollably, sending her into shockwave after shockwave of pleasure even as she wondered how bad the gunshot was.

She felt Destiny's seed filling her, felt her cock throbbing inside of her and it almost threw her off the cliff again. They stayed like that a moment before Destiny roughly pulled out of her, leaving her gaping wide and still pinned to the tabletop.

"You're lucky you wore a vest."

Lucia winced as Destiny's fingers probed the gunshot in her side.

"Redirected it down into the table, mostly."

"Good to know," Lucia panted. Yanking herself upward at the cost of ruining her jacket.

She stayed half-bent, bracing one hand on her side and the other against the table, cum and blood dripping on the floor between her still spread legs.

"So," Destiny zipped her pants back up and took a

nonchalant seat across from her.

She grabbed the bottle of wine from where it lay knocked over on the floor and took a long, deliberate pull.

"I have a job for you."

Esme

C. Quinn

B and I had a lot of nights that weren't very flashy. We'd take one of the bikes out, go to a dive bar, maybe shoot some pool. We dressed for the crash, not the ride, but fuck if her ass didn't still kill. Tight pants and a leather jacket - she'd complain about helmet hair and I literally wouldn't be able to hear her. It was impossible she couldn't see it.

Esme could see it. But I get ahead of myself.

One Thursday night towards the end of summer, I told B I was in the mood to take a ride and that she was to get ready for it after work. She did, setting out the riding pants and jackets we usually wore, waiting for me to fill in the rest. I had a late meeting and beckoned her in when she came to check on me. She spent the end of my meeting on her knees, eagerly trying to convince me to join her in the shower after my call ended. She knew what I wanted, she knew I couldn't talk to clarify, and her bratty ass took full advantage. Edging me with her throat and tongue over and over then scampering out of range just before I was able to end the call.

I picked her up in the shower and pressed her back against the cold wall, two things I normally don't do. I growled into her ear that she could come down when she'd done her job and her pussy clenched immediately. Gyrating her hips (fuck she's getting good at that) as I pounded her into the wall, I told her I could feel how wet she got sucking my cock. She whimpered that it was the shower and I chuckled as I gripped her ass tighter. I told her that she wasn't allowed to cum after all, holding her in place as she squeezed down on me, then groaned as her little body gave me the release I needed. She whined and pouted and tried to beg as I put her on her knees to clean me up.

I laid out a set of lingerie which I knew she'd soak through and a nearly see-thru top to go with the tight black riding pants. She whimpered again as I set out a heavier black leather collar to complete the look but she didn't fuss. She knew we'd be going to a local spot. Everyone there with eyes already knew she belonged to me.

The collar wouldn't share any secrets.

We left the Indian and took the Harley tonight. The way her hands moved on my abs told me that the heavy rumble between her thighs was keeping her in high gear, which was just fine. I wanted her that way.

The thing was, we'd been going on Thursdays to our local dive for a couple weeks now. I'd noticed a pattern, a girl I'd seen there the past three weeks, and I wanted to see if it would hold true. I had pointed her out to B last week. She'd gotten that dumb puppy look in her eyes, the kind of look that says 'yes please' to a treat. We hadn't said hi yet, but given the eyes this girl had made our way she definitely liked what she saw in one or both of us. If she was there tonight, it was time to put that to the test.

Walking in, I immediately noticed her. She'd set up at the table we were at last week, and she was checking her phone as soon as we walked through the door - trying to disguise that she'd been watching it. I wasn't fooled. I told B to go to our usual table, I'd get her a drink, and she answered "moving" before even realizing that it was occupied.

This would be fun, between how needy she was and how naturally she managed to be smooth with women - all the while thinking she had zero game. When I came back from the bar, B was still blushing a little, apologizing for almost not seeing our soon-to-be new friend.

"Who's your lovely friend, B?" I asked casually, setting down a pair of tequila sunrises and a whiskey coke double. Ashley, one of the servers who was both entirely in love with me and endlessly simping for B, set down three cold tequila doubles, limes and salt. She winked and blew B a kiss as she sauntered back to the bar. I could tell she was staring at the mirror behind the bar to see if we watched her walk away.

"This is Esme!" B beamed at me and tilted up her chin for a kiss, almost pouting for it. I gave it to her, deep but not overly long. "Let's not be rude, pet." I smiled at her and turned to Esme.

She hadn't looked away while we kissed and was blushing lightly, not overly easy to accomplish on a gorgeously tan Latina. I could see her shifting in her seat slightly, mouth slightly parted. I reached out a hand. As she offered hers I turned it slightly, half bowing and smiling at her. "The pleasure is all mine," I said as I introduced myself.

I glanced at the table. "Oh my, we've been overserved. Care to join us for a drink?"

She laughed a little at that, and I slid both a shot and one of the tequila drinks over to in front of her. She was definitely blushing now but she just nodded, still smiling. B beamed at her and said "next round we'll have to do it in a more fun way" with a mischievous little smirk. She clicked her glass against ours before tapping the table and tossing it back.

"Pool?" B grabbed both of Esme's wrists and pulled her along towards our usual table. I watched for a moment. Usually B asked me to rack, but either through her natural affinity or perhaps from watching us last week, Esme stepped to the end of the table and began doing it immediately. She was in a bright yellow romper. It was deliciously short and hugged the curves of her ass. Flowy at the top, it had a deep neckline that accented her natural assets. She made a vibrant counterpoint to B's black pants and lacy black lingerie shimmering through her top.

I almost didn't want to join them; spectating could

be such a pleasure. However, I thought I'd spice it up a little - so I changed the game to screw your neighbor. A shot for you if the last one of your balls went in. A double if you sunk your own ball and gave balls back to the other two. As we paced around the table, sliding past each other became grazing each other became, in B's case, an excuse to fully grind across her opponent, either myself or Esme - it quickly didn't seem to matter. She was getting that slightly glazed look in her eyes, breath coming a little heavier, blush rising in her cheeks a little faster.

I pulled her close on her next pass. I kissed her neck, and then softly told her. "You will need to go to the bathroom after your next turn - if you even get one. If she offers to go with you, say yes. You can help her with her romper, but you're only allowed to tease. If she tries to kiss or touch, you just point at your collar and say "we need permission" exactly that."

Her eyes were absolutely dazed but she nodded, a soft "Yes Sir" interrupted by Esme shouting a celebration as she sunk B's last ball. "A shot for youuuu" she exalted, pumping one hand in the air and then crooking a come-hither finger at B.

I got one from the bar and B told Esme to lean back. "You got me out you bitch!" She was laughing as she said it "...so you can make this fun for me." B traced a finger along Esme's collar bone down between her breasts to the low hem of her neckline, and then handed her the shot. Esme raised her eyebrows then tipped the shot glass as B leaned in, catching the liquid as it spilled along that route, chasing the last drops with her tongue up Esme's body...

"I think I need to go to the bathroom, now." B shot a look back over her shoulder at me and I nodded. "I'm coming too." Esme barely managed to squeak out, as B once again took her by the wrist and guided her through the bar.

The bathrooms here were single occupancy, but nobody stopped them. I swirled my drink for a moment and grinned, then sat back down at my table to see how well B was going to listen tonight.

———

As the door clicked shut B pushed Esme gently back against it. She traced a finger along the path the shot had traveled and smirked. "You're still a little sticky, honey."

The blush had spread to Esme's chest.

"Here honey. Let's get you out of that and you can go first." B slipped the romper off of one shoulder, then the next, moving slowly and deliberately, giving the girl more than enough time to stop her. Esme had on lovely little heels, giving her a couple of inches but she was maybe 5'3 even with that. She'd be eye level for B if she was barefoot, but with B in her boots the little thing was forced to look up at her while they were so close together.

B kept her hands on the romper and slowly slid it down Esme's body, revealing that she had only the barest strip of fabric covering her. There was no bra to complement the bright yellow thong she had on, and as she stripped down over her gorgeous ass the girl's hips bucked forward slightly. The wet spot was unmistakable. B took her in fully with her eyes, helping her step her heels out of the romper and guiding her past towards the toilet. She winked at Esme and said "just give a little shout when you're done and I'll come back in to get you dressed again." Esme pouted and stared hungrily as B sauntered out of the bathroom to plant her back against the door.

A minute later B heard her name trilled through the door in Esme's sing-song voice and she was quickly back into the bathroom. Esme's thong was in her left hand, standing there in her heels, legs slightly parted. She was smooth down there with a perfectly even tan and there was no mistaking the look in her eyes. "Going to help me get dressed, B?" She waved the thong lazily in a small arc. As B nodded and stepped forward, thong seemingly slipped from her fingers and landed on her foot, catching on the strap of her heels.

"Oops."

B smiled and leaned down, eyes not moving from Esme's perfect pussy as B's fingers traced the lower portion of her leg to retrieve the thong.

She could feel the other woman quivering. Her

fingers traced their way back up, nails scraping along her inner thigh, fingertips so close that she could feel heat before pulling back her hand. Esme whined in the back of her throat. B put a hand on her chest and pushed the shorter woman firmly backwards, invading her space more and more with small, intimate steps until her shoulders hit the wall. "For balance" she breathed, lips so close to Esme's ear.

Then she leaned down again and tapped first one foot, then the other, as she slid the thong back on. Hooking her thumbs to guide the tiny garment, she let her fingertips drag once more as she guided it into place. Her palm grazed against the front of Esme's panties and she felt the woman instantly grind back, but her hand was already gone as fleeting as a kiss. Esme groaned and B leaned in close again. "One more time honey." Her lips were a hair from the other woman's neck. B could feel Esme was nearly vibrating with frustration.

The romper was trickier, but she managed and as she pulled it back into place Esme grabbed her wrists. Her eyes were pleading, her thighs obviously grinding together. "Why.." she was searching B's eyes.

B lifted a finger, and tapped the front of her collar. "I want to honey. But we need permission for more."

Esme's eyes widened. "It's not just a fashion statement?"

B shook her head. "Oh no honey, I am His." She felt

Esme's knees go weak, saw her lips part as she audibly gulped.

The smallest "oh" was all she managed. B's smile widened. "Oh little one, he was so right about you. We're going to have so much fun... let's go get that permission baby."

"Don't you need to pee, though?"

"Oh no, I never did honey." And B grabbed her wrist and pulled her out of the bathroom, back to me.

From the way they moved back through the bar I could feel the mood had deepened. They'd locked into a similar rhythm, and B wasn't just guiding Esme anymore; their new friend was clinging to B. Both of their eyes sought me out, B grinning and Esme deeply red, but with that slightly glazed look to her face that said far more than words could.

I stood up as they approached. "Round 2?" The question hung in the air for a moment before I continued "or perhaps round 2 would be more fun at home?" Twin pouts changed in a moment as B nodded eagerly and Esme shyly, biting her lower lip and glancing over at B's enthusiasm.

"Too easy, we'll leave the Harley here tonight." I ordered an Uber and they tagged along at my heels as I went to the bar. We got another round of drinks while we waited, and I noticed how B's hands never seemed to quite leave Esme's body. She must be seriously revved up, I mused, contemplating what might have happened in the bathroom. I leaned in and kissed B against the bar, hard, as her hands trailed up and down Esme's back.

"I think our friend is getting a little jealous, love. Esme, do you want to kiss B too?" The pretty little thing could only nod, and I reached out to her and drew her between us, my hands gentle but strong on her hips. B's hands slid up her body to cradle her face, and as she kissed her, she pressed Esme back into my chest.

Esme tensed and then melted, and I could feel her body responding as she ground back against me. B's hands were not behaving at all, but cradled between the two of us it wouldn't have been too scandalous.

I leaned down, my mouth nearly grazing her neck. "May I?" And I felt her nod, heard her moan "please sir" around B's lips, as my own found her neck.

We stayed like that for only a few moments before I looped a hand around Esme's waist and pulled her back out of B's hands. "Let's get out of here before we get cited for indecency," I winked at them.

I guided them to the door where the Uber was just pulling up. Opening the door for first B, then stopping Esme and guiding her around to the other side of the SUV and placing her in the middle between us.

Another one of those adorable, quiet "oh" 's escaped her lips as she felt each of us lay a hand on her thigh almost in tandem. B's hand slid up her thigh and she leaned in close to Esme's neck. She was quivering under our hands and she turned to me and kissed me.

Hard.

And between breaths and moans she started begging. "Please sir, can we do more? Please I want her to be able to do whatever she wants and I... I want to touch you too." I could almost feel the heat coming off of her face, our lips still partially touching as she begged, both of her small hands fidgeting with the edge of my shirt, trying to pull it out of the way of my belt.

"Yes, little one." The words hardly escaped me before she was wrestling with my belt, and I felt her tighten up suddenly as I felt her thighs spread and I knew that B had been listening too.

"Let's behave ourselves a few minutes longer, lovelies. We're nearly home." My hand traced it's way up from her thigh, past B's skillfully moving hand and up her taut stomach, between her breasts, meandering to find its way on her throat.

I gave a firm squeeze, a gentle but steady tightening that echoed in her entire body. "You can be good for me and wait until we're inside, can't you?"

She nodded and moaned into my mouth. "That goes for you too, babydoll." B flashed her frustrated smile, such a specific expression, before pulling her hand from between Esme's thighs and giving her middle finger a long, languid lick.

"Sir, she's delicious though..." B whined, her eyes twinkling with mischief.

"We're turning down our street, love. We won't make the pretty little thing wait much longer," and I turned Esme to B whose lips eagerly took my place. I kept my grip there a moment longer, before relaxing my hand and feeling the deep heady breath relax her whole body.